MAY 1 5

PAPER THINGS

JENNIFER RICHARD JACOBSON

CANDLEWICK PRESS

First edition 2015

Library of Congress Catalog Card Number 2014944677
ISBN 978-0-7636-6323-0

14 15 16 17 18 19 BVG 10 9 8 7 6 5 4 3 2 1

Printed in Berryville, VA, U.S.A.

This book was typeset in Adobe Caslon.

Candlewick Press
99 Dover Street
Somerville, Massachusetts 02144

visit us at www.candlewick.com

For Don, for always

· 1 ·
SCORE CARDS

I sit up taller in my wobbly desk chair and try to tune back in to Mr. O. talking about supply and demand. At least, that's what he was talking about five minutes ago, before my mind drifted back, once again, to the night we left Janna's.

Janna, our guardian, had been on the phone with someone, tidying up the living room as she talked. "My daughter has always excelled," she'd said.

Gage had been passing through the kitchen, searching for his phone charger. I'd looked up from the breakfast bar, where I was studying the Pottery Barn catalog, to see if he'd heard Janna. Sure enough, I saw him give a little shake of his head.

He'd turned to me, but I'd quickly looked down, as if the decorative pillows needed my full attention. I didn't know if he was mad that Janna was bragging on me, that she had called me her daughter, or that she was pretending that nothing was wrong (probably all three), but my feelings were too much of a mishmash to give him the conspiratorial smile he was expecting.

When Janna hung up, Gage asked, loudly enough for her to hear, "Are you packed?"

I'd nodded, this time not daring to look at Janna. I hadn't packed much: my school uniforms, socks and underwear, a couple of weekend outfits, pajamas, a picture of our mother when she was a girl, and my Paper Things. The shoe box I kept my Paper Things in wouldn't fit in my duffel, so I'd carefully placed them in a double-pocket folder that I found in Janna's desk. Gage said I should pack only the essentials—that we'd come back for the rest later. But I'd overheard Janna tell Gage that "the rest" were things that she had purchased and therefore belonged to her.

"Is there laundry in your apartment building?"

Janna asked Gage. "Are you going to make sure that Ari has clean clothes for school?"

I kept my head down but sat perfectly still. I'd asked lots of my own questions about our new apartment, but so far my brother had been vague with his answers. Mostly he'd said, "Wait till you see, Ari! You'll be able to decorate *real* rooms in our place."

"Who do you think did her laundry before we came here?" he said, and then bolted upstairs to his room before Janna could say anything more.

"I should call Legal Services," she said, more to the air than to me. "I don't care that he's your brother. I don't care that he's nineteen. I'm sure they would agree that you should stay put." She paced, but she didn't call. Gage said that she couldn't call, because if the truth came out about how she'd treated him and how she was trying to keep us apart, she'd lose any chance she had of ever getting me back. Not that he planned on giving me back, he'd been quick to reassure me.

By the time Gage had returned downstairs — with my duffel bag and his backpack in tow — I'd finished with the Pottery Barn catalog and stood by the sink, as if waiting for a bus. As soon as Gage was within earshot, Janna turned to me and said, "Who do *you* want to live with, Ari?"

I'd been dreading that moment. For days the two of them had been battling, fighting to claim me, like I was a goldfish and not an eleven-year-old person who has her very own feelings.

But I was ready for it. I'd been practicing my answer: "I wish—"

"Don't do that to her!" Gage shouted, getting up in Janna's face. "Don't put her on the spot like that. You know she doesn't want to hurt you. But I'm her *family*! Not you. Me!"

"Your mother wouldn't want—" Janna started.

"Our mother said to stay together," Gage shouted. "Always! 'Stay together always!' Those were her exact words."

Janna had folded her arms and pursed her lips. It was a look that Gage often imitated to make fun of her—though I could tell that he was way beyond being amused at this point.

"Be reasonable, Gage. You're young. You've got things you want to do. Dreams for yourself. Do you really think you can do all of that while taking care of Ari?"

Once again, they were back to discussing me like I wasn't even there.

"What do you know about my dreams?" Gage yelled. "All you've ever cared about is Ari. And trying to make her love you. But guess what? She doesn't love you. She loves me. Her *family*."

Janna flinched as if he'd hit her.

I opened my mouth to say something, but no words escaped.

"Come on, Ari," Gage had said. "Time to go."

I begged Janna without saying a word: *Please, Janna, tell Gage you're sorry. Ask him to stay.*

Janna just stared at me, long and hard, like she was waiting for me to say my thoughts aloud. But I didn't—I couldn't—and eventually she went back to tidying the living room. "I'll see you soon, Ari," she said in her friendly voice. Like I was that runaway badger, Frances, who was going no farther than beneath the dining-room table.

I wanted to press a rewind button, but I wasn't sure how far I'd have to go back.

"Bye, Janna," I said as we walked out the door. I wanted to add "Thanks for being our guardian" or even "Love you," but I knew both of those things would upset Gage.

I'm pretty sure Janna didn't answer me.

Two blocks away from Janna's house, Gage cleared his throat. "Listen, Ari, there's something I need to tell you."

That's when I learned that Gage had lied.

We didn't have an apartment. Not yet.

We didn't have a home of any kind.

That was the beginning of February. This is almost the end of March. We still don't.

I look over at Sasha's desk—something I do about fifty times a day—but she's not in her seat. My best friend is, at this very moment, down on Walnut Street, acting as one of the safety patrol leaders. She's shy, but I know she's doing a good job. She'll smile at the kindergarteners who got overly attached to the previous group of patrollers, and she won't try to boss the second-graders who mouth back if you tell them to walk quietly. I know because we've been planning forever to be safety patrol leaders. It's one of the fifth-grade leadership roles. You have to demonstrate leadership to get into Carter Middle School. Now Sasha has a chance, lucky girl.

Two months of school to go and I still haven't been chosen to do any of the leadership jobs. Not safety patrol, not tutoring, not shelving books in the media center. And I *have to* get into Carter. *Have to.*

Only problem is, it's a school for the starry gifted, and I seem to have lost all my shine.

So I shake off thoughts of Gage and Janna and try again to make sense of the supply-and-demand diagram Mr. O. has projected onto the whiteboard. I give myself hooks so I can remember what it means. Supply is how much of something is available, and the more demand there is for something, the greater the supply will be. Like always, I think of the products in catalogs. You can always find watches, luggage, and sheets in the Macy's catalog, so there must be a steady demand for those. On the other hand, blue fuzzy slippers (like the ones Mama used to wear) and air popcorn poppers have disappeared—probably because the demand for those stopped.

"Can you think of something that has a big supply but no demand?" Mr. O. asks.

I know from the way Mr. O. has asked the question that the correct answer is no, but I can't help searching for an exception.

Cockroaches. Big supply, no demand. I start to laugh, but manage to stop myself by pinching my lips together. Still, a tiny choking sound escapes.

"Ms. Hazard?"

Now half the class laughs, as they always do when a teacher uses my last name. I've been in the same class with these kids since kindergarten; you'd think the novelty would have worn off by now. Holy moly.

"Perhaps you can tell us what's so funny?" Mr. O. says.

But rather than turning to me to see how I respond, the class turns toward the door.

Mr. Chandler, our new principal, has walked into the room. Unlike our old principal, who was friendly and knew me by name and was forever congratulating me on my school successes, this principal slinks from room to room like he's trying to catch someone in the act of wrongdoing. And sure enough, he has.

We are all frozen in position, staring at Mr. Chandler.

Daniel, a kid in my gifted class, gives my chair a subtle kick.

I turn back to Mr. O., who, despite the interruption, has kept his eyes glued on me.

"Sorry, Mr. O'Neil," I say.

I look down at the graffiti carved into my desk (not by me), hoping Mr. O. won't force me to explain what made me laugh.

He doesn't. Instead, he gives Mr. Chandler a little collaborative nod, which seems to satisfy the principal. The principal leaves, and Mr. O. continues.

"It seems to me, Arianna, that you don't have much room for fooling around."

I nod vigorously.

It's true; my social studies grade is the pits. I did lousy on both quizzes, and I haven't been able to finish the outline of my biography (along with a bibliography) on a famous nineteenth-century American. I'd promised it to Mr. O. today, but we had to meet up with West last night, so it was impossible for me to stop by the library to do my research. Without West, one of the social workers at Lighthouse, we can't sneak in, and Lighthouse is the only shelter Gage will stay at. I think we're at Chloe's tonight. That will make Gage *très, très* happy. (See, Mademoiselle Barbary, I am using my French!) It will make me happy, too. And maybe I'll even be able to get caught up on my homework.

I force myself to pay attention—to listen to Mr. O. talking about the poor imaginary bookseller who has bought a ton of books, but now nobody wants them.

I wish I hadn't laughed in Mr. O.'s class, I wish I hadn't been caught by Mr. Chandler, I wish I could be seen as shiny once again.

· 2 ·
MANUALS

Sasha is waiting for me on the corner of Walnut and Washington, still wearing her patrol leader vest over her red puffy coat. Today, her so-blond-it's-nearly-white hair is pulled back in a bun, like she has a ballet recital or something. All day, girls have been saying, "I like your hair, Sasha." No one has complimented me on my hair in weeks. Janna was the one who could do the French braids and cool updos, not me. And definitely not Gage.

"Patrolling is so much fun, Ari!" She's bouncing up and down like Leroy, the little terrier we had when Mama was still alive—four years ago now. I can remember Leroy's funny little face more than I can Mama's, which makes me feel terrible. Gage says that I shouldn't feel bad, that memories are strange that way . . . and besides, most people remember from pictures. We don't have many.

"Were you on walker patrol or bus stop?" I ask Sasha.

"Walker!"

"Wow! Really?" I was expecting Sasha to say bus stop. On bus stop patrol, you tell each line when it can board and help the little ones climb the steps. But on walker patrol, you have to gauge traffic and direct kids to cross at the precise moment.

"Did you have to determine the safe gap?" I ask. The safe gap is the time it takes for a car to get from the intersection to the crosswalk.

"Yup. But there are lots of other responsibilities, too," she says. "Like reminding bike riders to walk their bikes across the street."

I nod, but I also keep my eyes peeled to the sidewalk for pennies. People don't bother to stoop down and pick up the pennies they drop. You'd be surprised how a few pennies can start to add up.

We're on our way to Head Start, where I help out after school. West told me about the job; he knew I was looking for leadership roles and said the teachers at Head Start could really use my help. I didn't have the heart to tell him that the only leadership roles Carter was interested in were the ones our teachers assigned us. Besides, the job sounded interesting—and it gave me access to lots of free catalogs!

"Wait till you see the kinders," Sasha says. "They are so sweet!"

I've never heard her call kindergarteners that before. Maybe that's patrol leader talk. To tell you the truth, I never thought Sasha would be patrol leader before me. For the millionth time, I wonder if things would have been different if I'd stayed with Janna.

I nod. "Like the Starters," I say, trying out this new lingo. "They're cute."

"Sasha Skinny!" we hear Linnie yelling as she races down the hill toward us. She lives right here on Boyd Street. She stops fast, like she's on the basketball court and just caught a pass.

"Sasha Skinny!" Linnie says again. "I *cannot* believe you are safety patrol leader!"

Leave it to Linnie to insult Sasha while pretending to compliment her. Who better than Sasha to be patrol leader? (Never mind that just moments ago I was thinking how surprised I was that Sasha was chosen before me.)

Sasha pulls the vest off as if she were caught at the end of a first day of school still wearing a name tag with the Eastland Tigers on it.

"Ari should have been patrol leader," says Sasha quietly. "I'm sure she'll be next."

"Ari?" says Linnie, looking at me for the first time since she caught up with us. She singsongs, "I don't think so," then laughs.

"What's so funny?" I say. I know that Linnie isn't laughing because she's jealous; she doesn't want to be patrol leader. She didn't even bother to sign the interest form, since she already knows that she's going to Saint Anthony's next year. "I'll be patrol leader next. You'll see!" I look to Sasha to defend me.

"She will," Sasha murmurs. But instead of staring

Linnie down, Sasha's looking at the ground.

That's when I realize that Sasha's just being nice. She's no longer sure I'll be chosen. Or maybe she's no longer sure I *should* be chosen.

"I'll call you tonight," I say, and walk away.

3

CATALOGS

As soon as I go through the door of Head Start, Omar looks up. He leaves his spot at the water table and barrels into me the way little kids do, wrapping his arms around my legs, the water from his hands seeping into the back of my pants. The happy sound he makes is a cross between a fire truck siren and a guinea pig squeal. Other kids leave the centers where they've been playing and come trap me in a kid cocoon. None of them worships me quite as much as Omar does, but they all love to greet me in the same way.

Carol is on the other side of the room, pouring milk into little metal pitchers for snack time. "So glad you're here!" she calls, like she always does. I look around the room for Fran, but I don't see her.

Omar, who misses nothing, points to the drama center, the area underneath the loft. Today it's been set up to look like a grocery store. There are shelves with empty food boxes, a bin with plastic vegetables, and a toy cash register. Fran, who is so small she sometimes looks like she's one of the helpers, has a basket on her arm and is pretending to buy groceries. She says the word *potato* over and over: "Look, here is a potato! I like potatoes. I can't wait to get home and cook this potato. You can make French fries with potatoes." A lot of the kids in this class don't speak English, and that's Fran's way of helping them learn new words. All the teachers are big on repetition.

"Buy the po-po-tato!" says Marissa as she stands in front of the cash register, making it ring.

"Ari," says Juju, a serious three-year-old who always wears party dresses and talks in whispers, "go look in your cubby." Some of the kids return to what they were doing, but a small group pull on my fingers, leading me to my cubby, a painted wooden cube just like theirs. I know what I'll find, but I'm as excited as they are.

A small pile of catalogs greets me. "Count them!" the kids shout. They count to four with me, and then, for fun, we count them all over again.

Four catalogs! Two of them are for women's clothing, but there is the newest Pottery Barn, which will have pictures of furniture, and best of all, a Mini Boden catalog. In Mini Boden, all of the models are kids. I smile a thank-you at Carol.

"Is there a dog?" asks Omar, who, unlike the rest of the preschoolers, hasn't run over to get his carrots and graham crackers. We take a quick peek inside one of the catalogs, and sure enough, there is a dog. I think it might be a beagle. "Six dogs!" he shouts.

I place the catalogs on the cutting table and sit with the kids at Omar's table to have my snack. Carol has slipped me a hummus cracker sandwich. (The little kids don't seem to notice that my snack is different. Or if they do, they don't seem to mind.) As I take a carrot from the plate in the center of the table, I wonder if it's time to add a new paper family to the one I've already cut out.

I started my first paper family when Mama got sick. She spent a lot of time in bed, with books, magazines, and catalogs lying all around her. Sometimes she'd read to me, but when she got tired, she'd close her eyes and I'd look at the catalogs. At first I was just looking at the clothing, thinking, *Wow, wish I could buy striped puddle boots or a princess dress.* But eventually I realized that the clothes were laid out like paper doll clothes. That's how Sasha and I got the idea of cutting the people out and making paper families. (Back then, Sasha had been my downstairs neighbor, and we spent a lot of time at each other's apartment.)

In the beginning, there were just three people in my paper family—just like in my real family: Mama, Gage, and me. I started with the kids. You would think that finding pictures of kids to cut out would be easy, that I'd have a gazillion choices, but it's not true. Catalogs usually show only part of the model; most of the time their arms or legs have been cut off in the layout. In the first catalog I checked, which was an L.L. Bean kids' catalog, I could find only one decent picture of a boy. He looked like he was around seven, and he was crouched, playing with a lawn sprinkler. But he would do. I cut him out and named him Miles. In that same catalog was a toddler girl with dark hair and warm brown skin. She had on a yellow dress with leggings and was cupping a toad in her hands. Best of all, she was smaller than Miles—which was good, since I wanted her to be the younger sister. I cut her out and named her Natalie. Finding their mom was much easier. Most of Mama's catalogs were filled with women. I just had to find a mom that was about the right size: one who didn't fill up a catalog page and wasn't tucked in a tiny box in the corner, one who was the right proportion for my family. Luckily I found one who looked as fun-loving as my mom—before she got sick, of course.

While Sasha was choosing the people for her paper family, I decided to cut out furniture for mine. First I cut out a bed that was shaped like a boxy car for Miles. Then I found a white-lace canopy bed for Natalie. Later that day, Sasha went home and cut out furniture from her mom's catalogs. Before you knew it, we were creating whole rooms and outdoor patios and even parks with swings and slides and monkey bars. (The Home Depot advertisements that come in the mail have the greatest play gyms.)

My apartment was best for playing Paper Things. Since Mama spent so much time in bed, we would spread our paper worlds out across the floor of the living room. I showed Sasha that if you set up near a couch or chair, you could create an upstairs in your home. Sometimes Gage would complain that he was tired of stepping around scraps of paper everywhere, but mostly he just let us be. He was fourteen and we were seven, so he was probably glad we weren't bugging him.

I shake my head and focus on the four catalogs in front of me now. I tear out the pages that I don't want and set them aside for the kids to cut up. After snack is skills time at Head Start, and one of the skills the older kids learn is cutting with scissors. When I told Carol about Paper Things, she asked if I would be the helper at the cutting station. At first I thought I could teach the kids to make their own paper families, but it didn't take me long to realize that the best most of them can do is make scraps. However a few of them, like Juju, do an all right job cutting out shapes. Carol says I'm a good role model for them.

"Are you ready?" Juju asks. Omar might love me best, but Juju loves Paper Things as much as I do. She helps me throw away my napkin and paper cup and then walks me from the snack table over to the cutting station.

Omar comes, too, and reminds me to cut out the beagle for my family. My paper family has grown. Now there's a dad (one that looks so kind and strong—one that matches my image of my own dad, who was a war hero, but who died before I was born), four more kids, and five dogs. Six with the beagle. I've thought of starting new families instead of continually adding on to the one I have, but part of me wishes I belonged to a big family. With a big family you're likely to have someone watching out for you always.

"What should we call this dog?" I ask Omar.

He stops his own cutting (ripping is more like it) and looks thoughtful. "Let's call him —"

Claire sneezes.

"Gesundheit," says Fran.

Omar's eyes light up. "Let's call him Sneeze."

4

LIBRARY CARDS

"What do you need for homework?" Gage asks when he picks me up at Head Start. He's been working down at the docks today and he smells like fish.

"Library," I say, zipping up my winter parka. Some days now I walk around with it open, but it's more winter than spring tonight. "I need to research a famous American."

Gage sighs, though he tries to hide it. He's just come from downtown to pick me up. Now, since the library in the East End closed, he'll have to walk all the way back to the Port City library. "It will be easy to catch the bus to Chloe's from there," I remind him.

"Good point," Gage says, perking up a bit, and slides my backpack onto his shoulder. "Let's go, B'Neatie." Mama used to call me her Sweetie B'Neatie, and Gage uses the shortened version when he's in a good mood.

I hope, hope, hope that Mrs. Getchel is working tonight. She's the only librarian at the Port City library who's nice enough to look up your number on the computer if you want to take out books and you don't have your card. If you lose your card (which I did), you get one free replacement. After that, if you lose your card again (which I did), you have to pay for a replacement. It's only fifty cents, but I don't want to ask for it when I know that Gage, who is always worried about money, skips lunch.

Janna would say that I was irresponsible for losing my card (twice), but it's hard to keep stuff together when you move around the way we do. Besides, I'm pretty sure someone at Lighthouse took my replacement card when they lifted twenty-six cents from my pocket. Twenty-six cents won't get you much, but a library card will. A library card can let you borrow books, an MP3 player, and movies, or download materials on the computer. But you need to have an address to get a library card, and homeless people don't have addresses. I just hope whoever took it needed it—or really loves books.

You better hope they don't love books so much they don't return them, I imagine Janna saying to me. She'd be right. Then *I* would owe the library for those books. Even Mrs. Getchel wouldn't let me take books out if I owed heaps of money.

We stop at an intersection where cars whiz by, nearly splashing cold, salty slush on my legs. The light changes, and Gage strides out into the street. A man with a dog walks toward us. The dog, which I think is a German shepherd, isn't even on a leash— it just stays right next to the man as he walks. It isn't until the guy and his dog pass that I realize I know the man: he makes paper airplanes for kids at the soup kitchen. I didn't know he had a dog.

I watch them till they disappear around a corner and then keep my head down for the rest of the walk, scanning the ground for pennies.

• • •

As we climb the ramp that leads into the library, I tell myself that if I find one more penny, Mrs. Getchel will be working.

No penny.

Mr. Crowley and a woman I've never seen before are at the circulation desk at the library tonight. No Mrs. Getchel. My chest feels like I swallowed a gum ball whole.

I recognize more adults from the soup kitchen, snoozing in the comfy chairs. They've probably been keeping warm here since the shelters closed this morning. Mr. Hale, who says grace sometimes, gives me a little wave.

Gage marches directly to the *Maine Times* to read the want ads, like he does every time we come. He doesn't have a regular job but goes wherever someone needs him. Lobstermen are always glad to see him on fish market days. Tomorrow he'll probably be the dishwasher at the nursing home — Friday is the regular dishwasher's day off. He took me to work with him once when school was closed for the day, and I got to play bingo with the old people. It was fun except that one guy at our table, Mr. Lynnfield, kept cheating, and that made the other players yell at him. I felt sorry for Mr. Lynnfield — all that yelling at an old man whose hand shook every time he placed a chip. But when I tried to show him with my eyes that it was OK, that it was only a game, he winked at me. That's when I realized he liked the cheating . . . *and* the yelling.

I hope Gage finds a full-time job soon. What he didn't realize when we left Janna's is that landlords won't rent to you if you don't have a regular paycheck, no matter how much you've saved for the first and last month's rent.

I've decided to do my report on Louisa May Alcott, and I stop at a computer to see what the library has for biographies. It looks like there's at least one biography in the children's section and a few others in the adult section. I grab my backpack and head downstairs to the children's room.

Louisa May Alcott wrote a book called *Little Women* about four sisters and their "Marmee," which was what they called their mother. Janna read it aloud to me whenever Gage was out with his friends, which was a lot. It was funny at times and sad at times, and I kept trying to tell Gage about it, but he'd hold his hand up to stop me . . . suddenly needing to play closer attention to the music playing in his ears.

After I find the book, I grab one of the little pencils the librarians leave near the computer and begin to copy down information. Since I can't take the book out, I copy everything I can find on the title page and copyright page just to be safe. Next, I skim through the book, writing down the most important facts.

"What's taking so long?" Gage leans over my shoulder. "Don't do that here. Do the work at Chloe's."

My eyes instantly tear up. I feel like such a baby sometimes. "I can't take it out," I whisper. "I lost my library card again."

"Then, use mine." He opens his wallet.

I've never seen Gage borrow a book before. "You have a card?" I ask.

He looks at me. "Of course I have a card, Arianna. I can read."

"Well, yeah," I say, "but—"

Gage isn't listening to me. He's got that look on his face, the one he gets when he thinks someone is calling him dumb. Too dumb to get one of the college scholarships for foster kids. Too dumb to get a real job. Too dumb to be a reader. He grabs my book and hightails it up the stairs.

"Wait!" I say, too loudly for being in a library. Gage turns to look at me and I want to apologize, but all that comes out is "Can you take some adult books out for me, too?"

· 5 ·
PAPER DOLLS

The bus drops us four blocks from Chloe's apartment, and since it's getting dark, Gage grabs my arm. He hates this neighborhood. It's not the drunks he minds, or the bag ladies. It's the dealers, and they're not just drug dealers. Chloe has to pay a nine-year-old to protect her car. That is, she pays him so he and his friends won't slash her tires. I wonder what Gage would say if I told him that the same kid recently blocked me from getting on the number six bus to school. He wanted a dollar to let me pass. I told him that if he paid *me* a dollar, I would tell him how to get free doughnuts.

"Let's go!" the bus driver had shouted down to me. Everyone else had boarded.

I held out my hand.

The kid pulled a dollar out of his pocket and slapped it in my palm.

"I said, let's go!" the driver called down.

"Go to Mabel's," I said.

"Everyone knows Mabel's!" he yelled, grabbing my shirt as I started to climb the stairs. "And the doughnuts aren't free."

"They are if you tell Mabel that her cinnamon doughnuts are better than Dunkin's!" I said, and even though I could tell he wasn't sure if he should believe me, he let go.

I kept my eyes peeled for the kid, wondering what he would do if he saw me now. Probably he wouldn't do anything, since Gage was with me. But I wondered if my tip with Mabel had worked for him, or if she only gave me free doughnuts because she liked me — or maybe felt sorry for me.

There are always bikes parked in the entryway of Chloe's house, and a baby carriage. The carriage is probably used for groceries, though, since I don't think a baby lives in this building. As we climb the grimy stairs, I can smell natural gas from someone's stove and burnt cheese. I hope Chloe or one of her roommates is cooking tonight. Chloe (with newly dyed Twizzler-red hair!) opens the door before we reach the top of the landing.

"Hey, girlfriend," she says to me, but she's looking at Gage. They're like two supercharged magnets, and I slip past Chloe into the apartment because standing there while they kiss is just way too embarrassing.

Cody is standing in the little kitchen, microwaving Hot Pockets. "Hey, chica," he says. "Spicy Hawaiian or Four Cheese Garlic?"

"Spicy Hawaiian, please!" I say while dropping my backpack on the floor and sliding up onto a stool. I like coming to this apartment almost as much as Gage does. The kitchen and living room are one room, which if you watch as much HGTV as Janna and I did, you know is called *open concept*. It means that whether you're sitting at the bar in the kitchen area or on the fake-leather couch in front of the TV, you're always a part of the group.

Chloe's other roommate, Nate, is sitting in front of the TV now, playing a video game, but he gives me a nod.

There are two bedrooms—one off the kitchen end of the apartment and one off the living-room end. The one off the kitchen is Cody and Nate's. They have mattresses on the floor and these low, plastic drawers that, as far as I can tell, are never used; most of their clothes are on the floor.

Chloe's room has a bed, a black wooden bureau, and a desk. She also has a big closet, which is lucky, because she lets Gage and me keep some clothes and shoes there.

I wish that we could live here, but Gage said that the time isn't right. He and Chloe have only known each other for a few months, and he likes her too much to have the relationship move too quickly. (Before Chloe, he fell head over heels in love with another girl, Dominica, who turned out to be a big fat liar who broke his heart.)

But I like Chloe's a lot better than any of the

other places we stay, like at Gage's friend Briggs's tiny studio apartment on the West Side, or at Lighthouse, which is the only shelter we can stay at, because West doesn't make us fill out paperwork—technically you're supposed to be between twelve and twenty to stay there, so West has to sneak us in. I used to like staying at Sasha's, but lately I've felt weird about asking.

Unlike Chloe or Briggs or any of Gage's other friends, Sasha doesn't know that Gage and I left Janna's. I know it's wrong, wrong, wrong to keep secrets from my best friend, especially Sasha, who has *always* told me the truth, even when adults wouldn't or couldn't. It was Sasha who told me the meaning of words I knew I shouldn't say, and it was Sasha who, when we were playing Paper Things one day, made her little girl say to my little girl, "Oh, Natalie, your mama's going to die, you know." All the grown-ups around me kept sugarcoating Mama's hospital visits, but Sasha was the one person who told it to me straight—even though it was hard for her to say and even harder for me to hear.

I hadn't intended to lie to her about Gage and

me. The second night after Gage and I left, I called Sasha and asked if I could sleep over. All night I tried on different words to explain what had happened—what was happening—but I couldn't bring myself to say them. Partly because Gage had asked me not to tell anyone that we'd moved out until we got our own apartment. Partly because Sasha and I were having such a great time—applying oatmeal masks to our faces to give us clear complexions (Sasha had read about it in a magazine), designing what we were going to wear on the first day of school at Carter, and taking quizzes to find out our personalities—and I didn't want to ruin it. And partly because I was afraid to tell her. I still am.

After I eat my Hot Pocket, I go into Chloe's room to swap out the dirty clothes from my backpack and put in some clean ones. I'm actually really glad that we have to wear school uniforms at Eastland; no one can tell if I've worn the same uniform for three days—not if I'm smart about mixing up the shirts and the socks.

Chloe follows me into her room. "This one's

got your name on it," she says, handing me a towel. That might sound like she's telling me, "You stink, go take a bath," but I know she's not. The first few times we came here, I had Gage ask her if I could take a shower. I hate having greasy hair, and I don't usually take showers at Lighthouse because they're monitored. Now Chloe just offers first thing.

I head into the bathroom, and while the warm water pours over my head, down to my happy toes, I have fun imagining myself as Chloe and Gage's junior bridesmaid. If the three of us were a family, we could all live here together. Or even better, we could get our own place, just us. I can't imagine anything more perfect.

After my shower, Gage and Chloe tell me they're going to the Laundromat and ask if I want to come, which of course they know I don't. Besides, I have homework to catch up on.

"OK," Chloe says as I hand Gage my dirty clothes. "Feel free to take over my room."

I know that I should work on my famous-American outline, but I can't resist the urge to play Paper Things while I have Chloe's room all to myself. I reach into my backpack and pull out my folder. First I take out the things I found at Head Start. There's the dog, Sneeze, a farmer's table, and a beautiful blue bowl. I place my whole family around the long wooden table. The dad sits at the head of the table. When I was little, we had four chairs at our kitchen table. Gage always called one of the chairs "Dad's chair," even though Dad would never use it. I think that's one of the things he missed when we went to live with Janna. Isabella, the paper girl who is my age, carries in the blue bowl filled with ripe strawberries that she picked with her mother. Her mother who didn't die.

I remember the first time I played Paper Things at Chloe's place. I thought I was hidden in my little spot behind the couch, but Nate must have seen what I was up to, because he said, "You know, Ari, there's a dollhouse video game you could play."

"The Sims?" I asked. Janna wouldn't let us have video games, but I'd played the Sims at Linnie's house back when she was still my friend as well as Sasha's.

"Yeah, look," he'd said, pulling up a demo. Nate

was so excited about showing me the game that for a moment I thought I should pretend that I'd never seen it before. But then I decided he would be just as happy to go back to his own game, so I said, "I don't like the Sims as much as my own Paper Things," which is true.

"You're kidding!" he said, like it was impossible for anyone to like paper people better than electronic ones.

"In the Sims," I said, trying to get my words right, "the game decides what will happen to my families. If the Sims mom accidentally leaves the stove on, the house burns up. If a toddler falls into a pool, she drowns."

Nate stopped clicking and looked at me.

"I don't want to see that Grim Reaper guy," I added.

"Oh." He nodded, and I could tell he was thinking so much more than he was saying. "Good enough." He went back to playing his game, which was loud and full of violence. The very thing I don't like about video games is probably what makes them exciting for him.

Ever since then, I've avoided playing Paper Things when Nate or Cody is around unless I'm allowed to go into Chloe's room and close the door, which is rare. Now, though, I spread out my Paper Things on both the floor and Chloe's bed. My house has grown over the years. There are two living rooms and a playroom on the first floor, and five bedrooms on the second floor. Four of the kids share rooms, but my teenagers have their own rooms, and so does Nicky, who is the cutest little baby boy that I found in a Target catalog a few months ago.

When I first started playing Paper Things, Sasha raised her eyebrows at my family. My mom and Miles were white, my dad was Asian, and Natalie was African American. I'd just shrugged. "Not all families look the same," I'd said, and that seemed to satisfy her.

Before long, I'm lost in my world of Paper Things. My paper mom and dad are taking Miles and Natalie to the park, where they will meet up with their friends. Miles runs ahead to get a swing but trips and falls. Dad picks up Miles and carries him on his shoulders.

There are lots of voices in the other room, and I wonder if Gage and Chloe have returned from the Wash Tub. There's also loud music, and I pretend it's coming from one of my teenagers' rooms. "Turn it down, please," my mom says. (If it were Janna, she'd threaten to take the iPod away for a week, which is what she did to Gage—Gage, who lives for his music.)

I'm just about to start packing away my Paper Things and work on my outline when the door to Chloe's room flies open.

"Whoa! What's going on here?" says a guy I've never seen before who's about Gage's age.

"Careful! Don't step on her stuff!" There's a girl with him, and she wraps both arms around the guy's waist to hold him in place.

"Freaky," the guy says, and he backs out of the room.

"She's probably working on a school project," I hear the girl say. She closes the door behind her.

I quickly pull my things together and put them back in their folder, my face warm with embarrassment. "Freaky," the guy had said. I slide the folder into my backpack and pull out the library books. That's when I hear my name called.

Or at least I think I heard it. I open Chloe's door to find that the living room is filled with kids who I've never met. Most of them are drinking beer, and they're devouring a bag of Doritos. One of them offers me a handful, and I gladly accept.

The guy who thought Paper Things was freaky pulls the girl back into Chloe's room and shuts the door.

"Hey, Ari," says Nate. He pats the cracked couch cushion next to him, and I sit between him and a glassy-eyed girl who's staring to the left of the TV.

"Look what I found," Nate says. He's got his laptop, and he's pulled up an online clothing catalog that has lots of pictures of kids.

"They're the wrong sizes," I murmur, conscious of all the eyes on the screen.

Nate grins. "Watch," he says.

Of course! Because the images are digital, he can make the people any size he wants, although at some point they become blurry.

Nate and I are looking at the kids and guessing their personalities when Chloe and Gage return with garbage bags filled with clean clothes.

Chloe's face lights up. You can tell she's happy to see so many friends in her apartment.

"Hey, guys," she says. "What's the occasion?"

Gage pulls her closer to him. She doesn't notice, the way I do, that he's tense. Annoyed.

"Mason quit his internship today," says a girl with a pink gem in her nose.

"Finally," says Chloe. She pulls away from Gage, grabs a beer out of the fridge, and hands it to him, but he shakes his head no.

The door pushes open, and more kids flock through.

I want Gage to look at me, I want to give him a smile, to show him that this is OK, but he's looking at the crowd. "Get your stuff, Ari. We're going."

"What?" asks Chloe. Now she's paying attention to the creases on his face, trying to figure out what's made him mad. She makes a good guess.

"Ari's not a little kid, Gage. She's eleven. She's OK."

I give him my *please?* face, but it doesn't work. It hasn't worked much since we moved out of Janna's.

"Go on," he says to me. "Get your stuff."

"There's someone in Chloe's bedroom," I whisper. I know better than to barge in on them.

"Can you get her stuff?" Gage asks Chloe.

"My backpack is near your desk," I say.

Chloe doesn't move immediately. She just stands there and stares at Gage. Then she shrugs and tiptoes into her bedroom. I hope I grabbed all the clothes I need.

Chloe comes back out and hands me my backpack.

"You could come with us," says Gage. "We could hang out at Briggs's."

Chloe looks around the room. "Or we could stay here."

Gage takes the backpack from her and leans in for a kiss.

Chloe turns her face, but he kisses her on the cheek just the same.

I can hardly keep up as Gage hikes up the hill toward Briggs's apartment. "Don't go crabby on me, Ari," he yells over his shoulder. "I wanted to stay at Chloe's, too."

I'm not looking at him. I'm looking at the ground. It's really cold now, and my toes are beginning to feel numb. It happens all the time, partly because my shoes keep getting wet (my boots were stolen at Lighthouse) and some of the stitching is coming out. *Would Mama have been upset if I was at a teenage party?* I wonder. I know Janna would've been. I feel like telling Gage that he's just like Janna, but I don't.

When I don't talk, Gage talks more. "Things would only have gone downhill," he says. "Neither of us would have gotten any sleep there tonight. I have to work tomorrow, and you have to go to school." He's practically sprinting up the hill.

You're not my father! I feel like saying. But I don't. Instead I stay invisible. At least, that's what my silence feels like to me: I'm deep inside myself— with Gage, but not with Gage. I don't know why this helps me to feel better, but it does.

Gage stops to shout down the hill at me. "Even Chloe's room had been taken over! You have home-work to do tonight. You can't do homework in the middle of a party." He checks his cell phone and then quickly shoves it back into his pocket. No Chloe.

That's when it hits me: Chloe chose the party over being with Gage.

I race to catch up to my brother, and he drapes his arm around me as we cross Congress Street. "Tell you what," he says. "When we get to Briggs's, I'll help you with your school project."

"You will?" I picture Gage and me sitting at the little table in Briggs's studio apartment, and it makes me feel better. Maybe I will actually have more than an outline to hand in tomorrow. Maybe I'll get my paper completed by the April 19 due date! Maybe Mr. O. will have renewed faith in me, one of his supposedly gifted students.

It's not until we've actually reached Briggs's apartment in the West End and are letting ourselves inside with Gage's key that I remember.

I left the library books. The books we took out tonight. The books I absolutely need for my outline. Those books are about a mile away, sitting on the desk in Chloe's room.

· 6 ·
BOOKS

Briggs is assistant manager at the One Stop Party Shop, and his apartment is decorated with alligator party lights, smiley-face rugs, and dinosaur piñatas. It's a one-of-a-kind, coolio place. So staying at Briggs's apartment isn't that bad. That is, if you ignore the facts that it's on the opposite side of town from Eastland Elementary, has the grimiest, hairiest bathtub on the planet, and is a studio apartment— which means everything is crammed together into one tiny room—so I have to sleep on the floor.

Briggs has a matching love seat and chair. Both fold out into beds, which is *très* cool, but Briggs and

Gage, who are longer than me, get them. I get the seat cushions they toss off when unfolding their beds. Here is an ode to the seat cushions that I wrote in Language Arts last week:

ODE TO SEAT CUSHIONS

Oh, seat cushions
So quiet, so still, so nearly invisible.
Mindless occupants
Hurl themselves down on you
Unnoticing
The support you try to offer
The comfort you give
Your reliability.

But in my hands,
You are no longer reduced
To ignored decor.
You move from furniture to floor
And aligned triplets
Elongate
Turning lack into luxury.

You become my bed
Shielding me from
The foot-worn rug
Encrusted with Cheerios
Toenail clippings, and
Unvacuumed dead skin.

On you, I sink, I surrender, I sleep.

I am pretty proud of my ode. I had revised it
(You are no longer reduced / To ignored decor had
been *You are no longer a mere / Part of furniture)*, I
used some pretty decent vocab words *(aligned, elongate, encrusted)*, and I knew that the boys especially
would love the part about the rug being so gross.
But when Mr. O. asked for volunteers to share, I
didn't read mine. I thought of Gage and knew he'd
feel bad if I told everyone that I had to sleep on
a floor. And besides, I didn't feel like answering
questions.

Maybe I'll share it with Chloe, though, the next
time we see her.

• • •

I stay awake a long time worrying about Chloe. I don't want her to hurt Gage the way Dominica did—Dominica, who said that Gage was too clingy. With all his heartbreaks (one father, one mother, and three girlfriends), it's amazing he still tries to love.

After a considerable amount of time worrying about Chloe, I switch to worrying about Sasha. I'd forgotten to call her when we got to Briggs's. I knew she wouldn't try calling me at Janna's, 'cause she hates it when Janna answers the phone. (Sasha thinks that Janna doesn't like her, but it isn't Sasha that Janna doesn't like—it's Sasha's mother. But I'm not as good at telling my friend the truth, so I'd never cleared this up.)

And as if all that worrying hasn't kept me awake long enough, I worry about my books, and even worse, my bibliography. What am I going to say to Mr. O. tomorrow? Will he give me a big fat F? How am I ever going to get into Carter with bad grades? And how can I tell Sasha, with all our big plans of going to Carter together, that I got an F? Holy moly.

I guess I eventually worry myself to sleep 'cause an early-morning knock on the door wakes us up. It's

Chloe standing in the hall outside Briggs's studio with my stack of library books. She's holding them like they're really heavy, and she brushes her red hair off her face like she's put out by the journey, but she's wearing mascara and lip gloss, and I can tell (and I'm pretty sure that Gage can, too) that she doesn't want to leave things the way they were last night.

I would gush a thousand words of appreciation, but instead I thank her once and get out of the way quick so Gage and Chloe can make up. They go into the hall — supposedly so they won't wake Briggs, but I know it's mostly so they can have privacy. OK by me. I help myself to Cheerios.

"Who said you could eat those, runt?" Briggs says, crawling off his love-seat bed. I know he's only kidding. Of all of Gage's friends, Briggs is the nicest. Next year, when Briggs's lease is up on the studio, we might try to find an apartment that all three of us can share. Then Briggs would get to live in a bigger place, and the rent would be cheaper for me and Gage.

"Louisa May Alcott?" he asks, lifting one of the books Chloe brought me.

"Yeah," I say, glancing at the clock on his stove. It's a relief to have the books back, but I know that if I'm going to get to school on time, I still won't have an outline for Mr. O. And I can't risk being late again; one more tardy and I'll be assigned detention.

"You could choose any famous American and you chose Alcott?"

"She wasn't just an author, you know," I say. "She was an abolitionist and fought for women's rights."

"I know. I was gifted, too, remember?" Briggs likes to remind me of this. According to Gage, Briggs got into a bunch of good colleges but went to a nearby business school to save money. He's the first one in his family to go to college.

Which reminds me to get the coins I've collected and drop them into the piggy bank Briggs gave me. It's from One Stop Party Shop and is pink with daisies all over it. After I tap the coins in, I shake it like I always do. It's getting heavy. When it fills up, Briggs and I will take it to the bank, where they have a coin machine that will count your coins and pay you back in dollar bills.

"Hey," he says after the shake. "I brought you

something." Gage and Chloe come back into the apartment just as Briggs reaches into his closet and pulls out a hat that's shaped like an upside-down ice-cream cone. When you put it on, it looks like someone just turned a cone over on your head and the pink ice cream is running down your face. It's very funny, and we all laugh when he plunks it on my head, but it takes me a minute to realize why Briggs brought this hat home for me.

"We don't have Crazy Hat Day anymore," I say.

"What?" Briggs and Gage say at the same time.

"But it's an April Fools' tradition!" says Briggs. The first of April is coming right up.

"Yeah, Brigster," Gage says. "Remember when you wore that octopus hat and Mr. O. called you Calamari all day?"

Briggs laughs. "That name stuck for months! And remember how in third grade you came to school with all your baseball caps piled up on your head? Every year after, some kid tried to beat the record by wearing more. Heck, they're probably up to a hundred hats by now — that is, they would be if they could still do it."

"Mr. Chandler, our new principal, says that traditions like Snowflakes and Crazy Hat Day get in the way of learning," I say.

"Snowflakes?" asks Chloe.

The three of us explain that Eastland used to have all these cool traditions. At the sign of the first snowfall, the whole school would stop what they were doing and make paper snowflakes to hang throughout the hallways. In November, we'd hang homemade cards for the teachers, thanking them for all they do for us. Then at lunch, we'd have a big potluck feast that the parents made. And on April Fools' Day, kids wore crazy hats.

But the best of all the traditions, the one that we won't be doing for the very first time in the history of Eastland Elementary, is the fifth-grade campout in the library. Sasha and I had looked forward to this event for years. What could be cooler than sleeping over in the school with all of our friends and getting to see what the school is like at night, when it's dark and quiet and almost no one else is around?

But one of the first things Mr. Chandler did when taking over earlier this year was cancel all school traditions. We have to stay on task, our principal says. Which basically means if it isn't on a test, we can't do it any longer.

"Well," Briggs said, putting the hat back in the closet, "it's a shame. This would have been one cool crazy hat."

It's second period. I wrote up a rough sketch of an outline during homeroom and now I'm in computer lab, wondering if I can create my bibliography on the laptop in front of me without Ms. Finch noticing. Not an easy feat. Ms. Finch is the type of teacher who notices *everything*.

We're supposed to be exploring different sites that make word clouds. "Visual representations can be powerful," Ms. Finch says. I make eye contact so she thinks I'm following along. "What words come to mind when I say *community*?"

Paper Things, I think, but of course I don't say it. Instead, I open a blank document, pull one of the library books onto my lap, and begin typing the title and author, hoping the desk is doing a good job of blocking me.

Daniel, whom I've been determined to ignore since he dove onto the seat beside me—thereby forcing Sasha to sit on the other side of the lab—reaches over and grabs the book from my lap. I want to yell at him, but I can't risk alerting Ms. Finch, so I settle for a glare. I think he's just trying to get me to focus on my computer work, but instead he stretches over and starts typing on my laptop!

I try to brush his hands away, but I see that he's at the Port City library site and is searching for Louisa May Alcott. He clicks on the title of my book, copies the bibliographical information, and pastes it into my document. And just like that, I have all the information I need for my bibliography—with hardly any typing!

"Daniel?" Ms. Finch asks. I freeze. Have we been caught?

"Group, common, society," Daniel says calmly.

"Very good," Ms. Finch says, and moves on.

I let out a breath. Across the room, I catch Sasha's gaze. She rolls her eyes, as though Daniel was being a show-off. I smile at her, but secretly I'm grateful to Daniel. Doing my bibliography this way will save me a ton of time—and is less likely to get me in trouble with Ms. Finch, since I don't even have to take the rest of the books out of my bag. I know their titles and authors, and that's all I need for looking them up on the library's website.

As the rest of the kids are typing in words ("How do you spell *organization*?" I hear Linnie ask Ms. Finch), I look up the information for the next book. I'm careful to type only when everyone else is typing.

I'm getting close to the end—all the information is in place, but I'll need to fix the spacing before I turn it in—when Daniel reaches over and brushes his hand across my keypad, minimizing my bibliography.

"*Daniel!*" I snap. "Quit messing—"

"Ari," says Ms. Finch from behind me. Her wool pants brush against my arm. "Have you pulled up the class results?"

"Results?" I say weakly, but Daniel jumps in.

"We pulled up the results together. See?" He points to the word cloud on his screen. The word *community* is large and in the center. Around it are words in different sizes and colors, hanging together like a floating mobile. *Togetherness* stands out in large bold letters, almost as big as the word *community*.

Ms. Finch nods and moves on.

I glance at Daniel. "Thanks," I mutter, wondering why he's gone out of his way to help me—but too afraid of the answer to ask.

· 7 ·
HALL PASSES

"Come with me to the lab," I say to Sasha. "Please?"

"That bibliography was due ages ago," says Linnie. We're at the lunch table, and I'm trying to figure out how I'm going to get my bibliography printed and in my hands before social studies.

I ignore Linnie and continue to wheedle Sasha. "Please," I repeat. "It's my only option."

"Without a pass?" She's staring at me the same way her mother does anytime she thinks I'm luring Sasha into mischief.

"If we ask for a pass, the monitor will just say that Ms. Finch isn't there during lunch period. And that's the whole point."

Sasha sighs. I have never asked her to break the rules before. "Let's go," she says.

"Chandler will have your heads if you're caught," Linnie says.

I ignore her and wait for the monitor to walk over to one of the noisier tables. When he does, Sasha and I slip out of the lunchroom.

"Just act confident," I say to Sasha. "Like we have been asked to run an important errand."

"I'm pretty sure teachers aren't fooled that easily," Sasha says.

But when we pass Mr. Granger, our fourth-grade teacher, in front of the teachers' lounge, he says, "Hello, ladies," without stopping us — probably 'cause we used to be his best-behaved students. For a moment I wish I were still a fourth-grader.

Mademoiselle Barbary does stop us, but I say, "Computer lab," in such a strong, sure voice that she just nods and says, *"Vite, vite!"*

"See?" I say.

"Just go," Sasha says, nodding to the lab, up ahead.

Dim light behind the narrow window tells us

the room is not being used, but Sasha stops cold when I open the door to go in. The computer lab, with all the laptops and MP3 players, is probably the worst place in the whole school to be caught without permission. And we both have a lot to lose. I risk never getting a leadership role. Sasha risks losing the points she's made by being patrol leader. We could both end up with detentions, which stay on your permanent record. So much for Carter Middle School then.

I slowly open the door.

"I'm going back," Sasha says. Her face is a splotchy red, the way it always is when she gets nervous.

For a moment I consider going back with her, but I'm so close to being able to hand something in to Mr. O. . . . I nod OK and then slip into the lab. I wait for my eyes to adjust to the darkness, then I slide over to the laptop smack in the middle of the row ahead of me. I'm pretty sure it's the one I used. I hope it hasn't been powered down; Ms. Finch is the only one with the passwords for signing on to the computers again.

I tap the keypad and it wakes. I'm logged on, thank goodness, but I can't find my bibliography. I didn't get the chance to save it before Daniel minimized the window. But there are no open windows on my machine.

My heart sinks. I click on the trash can. Maybe someone deleted it?

"Is this what you're looking for, Arianna?"

It's Ms. Finch, standing in the doorway with a sheet of paper in her hand. The light is dim, but I know she's not smiling.

"I think so," I say, guessing it's my bibliography. My hands are shaking.

"You know," she says, coming over and shutting the laptop, "I wasn't born yesterday. A blank desktop tells me that a student has been perusing the Internet, that she's been doing something she wasn't supposed to be doing."

"I wasn't on a restricted site—"

"No, you were doing your homework for Mr. O'Neil during *my* class time. You felt his assignment merited your attention more than mine."

When she says this, it sounds worse. Worse than

goofing off, worse than looking at stuff we're not supposed to. It sounds like I don't think she matters.

"I must say, I'm very disappointed in you, Arianna," she says before I can figure out what to say.

Suddenly I feel the urge to tell her everything—about leaving Janna's and hopping from place to place. About leaving the books at Chloe's and struggling to find the time to do my homework. But I can't betray Gage. Besides, Mr. Chandler instituted a "no excuses" policy this year, and I don't want to break that rule, too. So I just stay silent, wishing I actually were invisible.

"Get yourself back to the cafeteria now," she says, dismissing me, "before someone catches you without a pass."

I nod and hurry to the door before she sees my tears. Ever since we left Janna's, nothing has gone right. It's starting to feel like the year when Mama died all over again.

We have a substitute teacher in science class, which is almost like having a snow day. No one bothers to pay attention, to do any real work. Lots of kids are talking, passing notes, even reading, in class. The sub doesn't seem to care. She just draws a cell diagram on the board and explains what she's drawing as if every single one of us found the structure of cells more interesting than juicy gossip.

I put my head down on the desk. The wood feels cool on my cheek.

"Do you feel all right?" the sub asks as she hands me a sheet of paper.

I sit up again and shrug. I can't stop thinking about my next class: social studies. What am I going to tell Mr. O.?

Maybe I don't feel OK. Maybe I'm sick. Maybe I should head down to the nurse's office. I think of lying on the green cot, the white cotton blanket draped over me. In the nurse's office, there's nothing more to do than watch the hands on the clock tick around.

Yes, I'm definitely feeling sick. I gather my courage to say so, but just then, the bell rings and kids swarm like bees out the door and into the hall.

I let the crowd carry me—all the way to social studies. Mr. O. is standing at his desk.

"Mr. O'Neil," I whisper as I approach him. What can I even say? I'm not allowed to make excuses, but if I just tell him I don't have my assignment—again—he'll think it's because I didn't even try to get it done.

Mr. O. picks up a piece of paper and waves it at me. "I was very glad to see this on my desk today, Arianna."

I look down. He's holding my bibliography. My bibliography, with my name at the top and the spacing corrected.

"Now that you have your sources, let's see if you can't get the outline to me, too," he says.

I keep staring at my bibliography.

"Ari?"

"Oh, I have my outline," I say, reaching into my backpack. "It's not typed—"

Mr. O. looks down at my outline and to my amazement nods in approval. "Looks like an interesting paper, Arianna, especially this section on activism. Do you think I might see an introduction soon?"

"Soon!" I say.

"Promise?" he asks, a little too loudly.

"Promise!"

How did this happen? I wonder, but I think I know.

I recall the word cloud we made in computer lab. What were some of the most prominent words? *Togetherness* and *help* and *support*. I decide that I'd also add *kindness*. And another word, which I'd type in ten times to make it stand out bigger and bolder than the rest:

Daniel.

· 8 ·
PRICE TAGS

"So, how is it being patrol leader?" I ask Sasha when I meet up with her after school. What I don't say is *Ms. Finch caught me in the computer lab and I think I might be in serious trouble* or *Daniel turned in my bibliography and really saved my behind, but I think the only reason he did it is because he feels sorry for me.*

"The best part is getting out of school early," she says.

"And the kinders," I prompt, smiling at the nickname.

"Yeah, they're OK," Sasha says. But she doesn't sound as excited as she did just yesterday. I wait for her to tell me what's changed, but she remains quiet.

"Oh, I almost forgot!" I stop and pull two math sheets out of my backpack. I hand one to Sasha and slip the other one down between my Paper Things folder and my science journal.

She moans. "Fractions and decimals *again*?"

"Want some help?"

"Please! I don't get them," she says. "Especially their relationship."

"Why don't I spend the night tomorrow night, and I could help you then?" I suggest, hoping my voice sounds natural, casual. It's easier on Gage when I stay with Sasha. He can get into Lighthouse without West sneaking him in, and his friends don't seem to mind as much when it's just him crashing at their place. Maybe he and Chloe can even have a date night!

She pauses. "Or we could stay at Janna's."

My stomach lurches. "I thought you didn't like it at Janna's that much," I say, hoping this sounds like the logical reason for not inviting her over for months.

"She rents the best movies," Sasha says.

"Forty-eight-hour rule," I say, sighing with what

I hope sounds like regret. I always used to hate this rule of Janna's—that she needed at least forty-eight hours' notice before a guest came over—but now I'm grateful for it.

Sasha sighs, too, though hers sounds less regretful and more frustrated. "I'll ask my mother if you can come over *again* tomorrow night."

"Great!" I say, trying to ignore the emphasis.

"Call tonight after you ask," she says.

"OK," I say, hoping she won't wonder why I'm calling on Gage's phone again.

Even though I know that Sasha is a little bit resentful about having to ask her mother if I can stay over *again,* all I can think of at this moment is that extra twin bed in her room, with the puffy comforter and clean, crisp sheets.

Heaven.

As I cross the road to Head Start, I see the airplane man from the soup kitchen sitting against a brick apartment building. He's got his arms wrapped around his dog, his chin resting on its head. The dog lifts its head and wags its tail as I come closer.

If Janna, the Queen of Rules, as Gage likes to say, were with me, she'd pull me away and remind me never to speak to strangers (rule number 72). But I've seen this man lots of times at the soup kitchen, so he's no longer a stranger to me. Besides, the dog is looking at me with its big brown eyes, and all I can think about is Leroy, our old terrier.

"May I pet him?" My voice wobbles a little. I've never spoken to the airplane man before, not even to ask for a plane. Guess I felt that I should have outgrown them—the way I probably should have outgrown my Paper Things by now.

He nods and I reach down and touch the soft brown fur between the dog's ears. The dog reaches its nose out and nudges the palm of my hand as if to say, "More."

"What's his name?" I ask.

"*Her* name's Amelia."

Amelia smells funky, like Leroy used to when he went too long between baths, but I move my hand all the way down her back just the same.

"Poor girl hasn't eaten today," he says, rubbing his hand up and down his beard, like his chin itches.

"How come?"

"Some days food's just a little harder to come by." Amelia rolls over to show us her tummy. She's loving the pats.

"The soup kitchen doesn't allow dogs, right?" I ask.

He nods, looking at me more closely now, like he's trying to place me. "Right. But even if they did, dogs need food that's made for a dog," he says. "Or eventually they get sick."

Poor Amelia. I reach into my coat pocket and touch the coins I've collected today. They're more than just found money; they're my way of showing Gage that I can help. But then I look at Amelia's eyes, and I swear my stomach does a flip-flop.

"Here," I say, holding out the fourteen cents. "I know it's not much, but if you keep looking, you might find enough to buy a can of dog food. A can of Alpo only costs fifty-two cents at Walmart." I know because I was cutting cans and boxes out of the mailer last week to tuck behind my paper cabinets.

"You seem to know a lot of things," he says. "What's your name?"

"Ari. Short for Arianna."

"Thanks, Ari. But I can't take your money."

"It's OK," I say. "I'll feel better if I know Amelia isn't hungry."

"You're a good kid," he says, and lets me drop the coins into his palm. Just then, I hear my name called from across the street. It's Carol at Head Start, and she's holding the door open for me.

"I better go," I say, giving Amelia one last pat.

"Next time I see you, Arianna," he says, "I'll have an airplane with your name on it."

As I stand on the edge of the sidewalk, waiting for a break in the traffic, I place my hand in my empty pocket. *It's OK,* I tell myself. *I'll search for pennies for twice as long tomorrow.*

"Do you know him?" Carol asks as I pass through the door, but before I've had a chance to answer, she asks if I wouldn't mind putting up a bulletin board in the front hall. She explains that she'd like me to staple up yellow construction paper with a lime-green wavy border all around the edges, and purple letters that say, WELCOME, SPRING! The board is high, so I have to stand on a small step stool to reach. It's actually kind of fun, and I feel like one of the teachers today instead of one of the kids.

Carol goes back inside the classroom, and Fran pops out.

"What do you think of these?" Fran says, carrying out some artwork the kids just finished. She's holding pussy-willow pictures made from brown paint blown through a straw, with little pieces of cotton ball glued on.

"Oh," I say, climbing down from the stool and touching one of the little fuzzy balls with my finger. And then my eyes sting with tears the way they do at the most ridiculous times. *Think of spring sunshine, think of petting Amelia, think of anything but pussy willows.* But it doesn't work. A tear rolls down my cheek.

"My mom made these with me," I explain to Fran, who is bending toward me, her eyes searching, trying to see into the secrets of me. But she doesn't hug me the way Carol would.

"Maybe you would like to come inside and make a picture, then," she says.

"That's OK," I say, sniffling and smiling to show

that things really are OK. "Do you want me to put these on the board?"

She nods. "But start with the drier ones," she says. "Or else we'll have brown paint and glue dripping all over your yellow paper."

I staple one of the pussy-willow pictures to the board and wonder what Mama would say about all the lying I seem to be doing lately. 'Cause the truth is, she never made pussy-willow pictures with me. Not ever. Janna did.

Janna used to do all kinds of crafts with us. She would spread a plastic tablecloth on the dining-room table and line up all the art supplies. Then she'd instruct us, like a teacher, on what to do first, what to do second. I was always happy sitting in my chair, wearing one of her old shirts for a smock, following her instructions. "Now take a teaspoon of brown paint and place it on your blue paper near the center. Not that much, Gage. Less! Less!"

I'd take my straw and gently blow the paint into a long, graceful stalk. Gage would blow too hard, causing the paint to run off the paper and onto the tablecloth.

"Gage, stop it!" Janna would shout. "Go grab a sponge and clean up your mess."

"Why does everything always have to be *your* way?" he'd ask.

"Because I'm the grown-up," Janna would say.

"Well, when I'm older, I'm only going to do the stuff *I* want to do," Gage would invariably counter.

"Not while you're living under my roof," Janna would say, and then Gage would stomp off, forgetting all about the sponge and leaving Janna to pick up his mess.

After a while, Janna gave up craft time. Gage didn't want to come to the table, and I didn't want to do anything without Gage.

I think about pussy willows. How little fuzzy pearls bloom from sturdy, straight sticks. How they burst open just when you've had way too much winter, promising spring.

I look down at the artwork spread out on the floor. Some pictures look like pussy willows against a blue sky; some look like poodles rolling in a mud puddle.

"Here, Ari." It's Omar. He's standing in the hall

next to Carol, holding out a newly painted pussy-willow picture. "I made this one for you."

It's messy. The paint is streaming in unexpected directions, and the cotton balls are gloppy with glue.

"I love it," I tell him. And I do.

· 9 ·
APPLICATIONS

"They want someone with experience," says Gage. He and Briggs are sitting on Briggs's love seat, looking at Briggs's iPad.

"Maybe they'll train," says Briggs, who is trying to be patient, but I can tell he's sick of Gage coming up with a reason for not applying to every job. I know, and Briggs knows, that it's not that Gage doesn't *want* to work—he works harder than anyone. And he really, really, really wants to get a job so we can get an apartment. It's just that he hates it when he asks and people tell him no.

I look up from my math homework. "Who's hiring?"

"Jiffy Lube," says Briggs. "It's a service station—for cars."

"They want someone with experience," says Gage.

"How do you get experience?" I ask.

"By working at a service station," says Gage.

"How do you work at a service station?"

"By having experience," says Gage.

The circle game has become one of Gage and my favorite games. All of our longings are trapped in circles where there is no beginning and no end.

"Hey," Briggs says. "It just occurred to me—my boss's brother owns a Jiffy Lube."

Both Gage and I look at Briggs like he just found a trapdoor.

"Do you think it's this one—the one that's advertising?" Gage asks.

"I don't know," says Briggs. "I could ask. No matter what, I could still tell him about you."

"Couldn't hurt," says Gage, letting his eyes speak a world of thanks.

We leave it at that and don't say anything more

about a job tonight. Hopes are as delicate as butter-
fly wings: say too much, want something too much,
and they'll crumble. Instead, I tell Gage about staying at Sasha's tomorrow night, which makes him
très happy. Then we both make phone calls—me to
Sasha, Gage to Chloe.

Suddenly the evening feels a whole lot lighter.
Briggs suggests we cook up some spaghetti and
meatballs. Gage insists on a veggie, too. I open
Briggs's freezer and choose green beans.

"Did you know," I say, after we've cleared our plates
and Gage has started on the washing, "that Louisa's
first book, *Flower Fables,* was published by George
Briggs? Maybe one of your relatives knew Louisa
May Alcott!"

"Oh, yeah?" Briggs comes over and sits at the
table with me. He takes my wrinkly Paper Things
folder out from the stack of books.

"Aren't you gonna play with your paper dolls?"
Briggs asks.

"I can't," I say. "I need to write an introduction."

Anyway, I know from experience that there isn't really enough room at Briggs's for me to spread out my whole paper world and not have it stepped on.

He opens my Paper Things folder and pulls out one of my kids.

"Who's this?" he asks.

I tell him her name, but I keep my eyes on the book in front of me. It's my way of telling him I can't be distracted right now.

"And who's this?"

"That's Miles."

"Wow, Miles has seen some miles."

I laugh. It's true. I've had Miles since the year Mama was dying. He's a thin scrap of paper, wrinkled and faded.

"What's this?" Briggs points to the sprinkler at Miles' feet.

"It's a sprinkler," I say with my *we're done now* voice.

"Wow, that's water spraying around. I couldn't tell. I thought it was just more creases in the paper."

He rummages through the folder, and I'm

afraid he's going to ask me about each item and every person in it.

I yank the folder out of his hands and place it at the bottom of the pile of books. He's still clutching Miles, though.

"Give," I say, making a grab for him.

But Briggs pulls his arm back playfully. And as quick as that, Miles tears in two.

I can't believe I'm only holding half of him in my fingers. Miles was the first person I ever cut out of a catalog. I have played with him in our apartment on Crest Street, at Sasha's, and Janna's, and every place we've stayed since.

My eyes don't tear up. I don't say anything. I'm more invisible than invisible.

"I'm so sorry, Ari," Briggs says. "I didn't mean to—" He jumps up and opens the kitchen drawer and comes back with tape.

"Let's fix him," he says.

I nod, but I'm pretty sure it's not going to make me feel better. Try as you might, there are some things you just can't mend.

· 10 ·
LOVE LETTERS

I arrive at Sasha's around three the next day—right after her dance lesson. A visit to Sasha's house always begins with a snack at the kitchen table. Today: kiffles, which are these *très* yummy Hungarian cookies that Sasha's mom makes with apricot jam filling.

"Are you still working at Head Start?" Sasha's mom—who I call Marianna—asks me.

I nod, my mouth too full of kiffle for me to speak. Flaky crumbs float down to the diamond-patterned tablecloth below. I brush them away as discreetly as possible.

Marianna blows on her tea. "Did Janna get you that position to plump up your application to Carter?"

I take my time swallowing. How can I explain how I got it without telling them about West and letting on that Gage and I no longer live with Janna — that we no longer live *anywhere*, really?

But Marianna doesn't even wait for an explanation. "Have you submitted your application?"

"No, not yet." But then I wonder: *How will I apply to Carter if Gage and I don't have a permanent address?* He'd promised me that it would only take us "a week, maybe two, tops" to find a place. But it's been nearly two months, with no end in sight. "When is it due again?"

"At the end of April," says Marianna, jumping up to look at the calendar on the wall. "There's still plenty of time to add new activities to your application," she reassures me.

"Like patrol leader," says Sasha, "or lunchroom monitor."

I try my best to smile. Between missing so many homework deadlines and getting caught by Ms. Finch, I wonder if I'm even still in the running for a leadership role. I wonder, too, how you even get an application to Carter. Are they automatically sent to the homes of the top-ranking students — of which I'm still one, though just barely — or do you have to contact Carter to get one?

I take a sip of my water and try to appear nonchalant. "I think I might have misplaced my application, but I'd rather not tell Janna if I don't have to. Do you know how I can get a new one?"

Marianna smiles and pushes the cookie plate toward me. "Sure, you just have to request one."

"From Carter?" I ask, taking another cookie from the plate. Marianna likes feeding me. Sasha can be a picky eater, but I'm not.

"No, Eastland Elementary has plenty. I had Sasha pick one up from the office."

Sasha rolls her eyes. "OK. That's enough about Carter, Mom."

"I was just answering Ari's questions, dear heart," Marianna replies. "Speaking of questions, have you started in on the student ones yet, Ari? Sasha here has been dragging her feet for weeks."

"Student questions?" I ask.

Sasha groans while Marianna goes to a drawer in the other room and returns with a manila envelope. Inside are notes she's kept from Eastland Elementary, copies of Sasha's report cards, a letter from Sasha's dance teacher. She shows me the application to Carter that she has begun to fill out. I glance down at the spaces to be filled in, and my head fills with its own questions: *What will I do if I don't have an address? Whose name should I write for name of parent or guardian? Should Gage fill out the parent questionnaire?*

Marianna turns to the third or fourth page of the application and points to the heading: Student Questions.

"Mom's made me practice answering them over and over," says Sasha. She gets up and moves to the kitchen counter, pretending that the edge of the counter is a ballet *barre*. "But I just don't feel like writing essays in my free time."

I read:

How would other people describe you?
What is the greatest talent or gift you would bring to the Carter School community?

Is there anything you would like us to know about
you that hasn't been shown elsewhere in the
application?

"You haven't started on these yet, Ari?" I can tell that Marianna is just trying to be helpful, but her anxiety is making *me* anxious, too. What if I've already waited too long to start filling out my application? Heck, I can't even manage to finish my introduction for Mr. O., and that's only a few paragraphs!

"Enough questions, Mom," Sasha says.

But Marianna doesn't seem to hear her. Instead, she reaches for the hairbrush that's kept handy in a kitchen drawer and begins braiding my hair—an event as common as our afternoon snack. Sasha won't let her mother fuss over her, but I love it. "Janna does realize how important it was to your mother that you attend Carter, doesn't she?" Marianna says.

I nod. Janna knew all too well just how badly Mama had wanted me to attend Carter. How many times had Janna tried to tell me to go easier on myself, that I should only push myself to get into Carter if it was something that *I* wanted for myself? And how many times had Gage blown up and said that my getting into Carter had been one of our mom's dying wishes, and how dare Janna try to interfere with that?

Everyone in my family went to Carter: Mama, my dad, Gage. Even Janna had gone. That's how she knew Mama. Back when they'd all gone, though, it hadn't been a school for the gifted. Gage didn't even have to apply; you were automatically accepted if your parents had attended Carter. Mama always said that the happiest times in her life were at Carter—except for having us, of course. And once it became a school for the gifted, she was even more adamant that I attend. "The perfect place for my smart daughter," she'd called it. It was like as long as she could imagine me somewhere that she knew well, somewhere that had belonged to *her*, I'd be OK.

"Enough, Mom!" Sasha cries. "Come on," she says, pulling me out of the kitchen and down the hall to her room.

When we get to Sasha's room, I start to take out my math folder, with a surprise for Sasha.

"Your backpack is always as fat as a Thanksgiving turkey. What do you keep in there?" Sasha says.

"Homework, for one thing!" I say, finding the folded sheet of paper I was looking for. "Let's do your math work sheet."

Sasha flops onto her bed. "Not now. Let's do it tomorrow!"

But I can't wait to show her what I've written. "No, really. You'll like this," I say. I unfold a letter, climb onto the spare twin bed, and read it aloud in my sappiest, lovey-dovey-est voice:

Dearest Decimal,

For too long, ma chérie, my heart's been shattered to pieces. (Sometimes in fourths, sometimes in thirds, sometimes in fifths—but always in pieces.) In this I thought I was truly alone. But then you came along, dear decimal. You, fragmented one, are my true math mate.

Sasha looks at me like she can't figure out which planet I came from.

I keep on reading:

Together with my solid little line and your petite point, we can express our sameness perfectly. I say 1/10, and you say 0.1. I say 1/100, and you say 0.01. I say 1/1000, and you say 0.001.

"Look," I say, pointing to the numbers in my letter. "Even though they can be read the same way, the fractions and the decimals look different. But you can see the pattern, right?

Sasha just squints her eyes at me, so I go on reading.

You and I have a complex relationship, but let me start with our most basic compatibility. We both express ourselves easily within a system of ten. As we move to the left of your decimal point, each place gets ten times bigger (like my love for you): ones, tens, hundreds, thousands.

When we move to the right of your decimal point, each number gets ten times smaller (like our decreasing misunderstandings): tenths, hundredths, thousandths.

And I? I can be a decimal fraction! A decimal fraction has a denominator (bottom number) that is 10, 100, 1000 (in other words, a power to 10). So if you want to waltz as 0.4 (four-tenths), I will glide as 4/10. And if you rock as 0.372, I will roll as 372/1000. What could be more divine?

Forever yours,
Fraction

P.S. I know that life is full of complications: there are improper fractions and the need to reduce from time to time, but we'll get through these new phases, I promise.

I look up, expecting to see a sky-wide smile on my best friend's face, but instead, she looks like Janna did whenever I accidentally walked into the kitchen with my shoes still on.

"When did you write that?" she asks.

"This morning after breakfast."

"Instead of working on your *own* homework?"

"Well, yeah. I wanted to. . . . I thought it would be a fun way to help you understand."

"A fun way to show off, maybe," she says. She shakes her head like I'm the one who's having trouble getting things. "Why do you have to do things so *weirdly*?" she asks. "Why can't you just sit down and show me how to convert a decimal into a fraction?"

"I can," I say, slipping off my bed and moving next to her. I tuck the words *show off* and *weird*, which have the weight and sharpness of scissors, inside an invisible pocket, where I can take them out and examine them when I'm alone.

"You know," she says. "I'm doing everything I can to get into Carter. What would help me the most is if you would keep trying, too. I don't want to go off to middle school all by myself, Ari."

That's when I realize that she is as nervous about next year as I am. "I'll get in, Sash," I say. "Trust me. One way or another, I'll do it."

Later, as we dance together in front of the TV, I think about Sasha's concerns. What would it be like for her to get into Carter and for me to have to go to Wilson? It would probably be the end of us; no one from Carter really hangs out with anyone from Wilson. Besides, Sasha would probably make a bunch of new friends—even though I know she's scared she wouldn't. Me, on the other hand . . . I don't like to think about what next year will be like for me if I don't get into Carter and Sasha does. Not only would it mean the end of the longest relationship in my life except for with Gage, it would also be the last little part of Mama—her dream for me— gone forever.

But how am I going to keep my promise?

"Keep up!" Sasha yells, swinging her arms like the dancer on the screen.

I vow to work harder.

But for now I have to focus on making things better with my best girl. "Hey, Sash," I say when the music stops and we have collapsed on the floor. "I have something else to show you."

"Not another letter," she says, following me back into her room and getting up on her bed.

"Nope." I go over to my backpack, take out my folder, and bring it to her. "Remember these?

Remember when we used to spend hours cutting things out?" Part of me knows I should have outgrown this game, and that's why I haven't suggested playing with them together since the beginning of fourth grade. But right now I just want to remind Sasha. I just want to make things right between us.

Sasha carefully pulls one of my teenagers from the left-hand pocket. "I remember her," she says. "I remember how she used to go to dances and was on the field-hockey team."

"Yeah," I say. "Look here." I open the pocket on the other side. "I still have all the furniture, too. And then some!"

Sasha reaches in and pulls out my yellow-flowered couch and a refrigerator. "I remember when you got this couch. I was so jealous. My couch was green-and-red plaid."

"It's hard to find whole couches."

"And here's Natalie's canopy bed," says Sasha. "I always wanted a bed like that. Still do."

"Remember how you had all those twins?"

"Yes!" She falls back on her bed, laughing. For some reason Marianna got two of every Lands' End catalog. Sasha loved cutting out duplicate kids for twins.

"Yeah, and then you gave me another catalog and I had triplets, too!" she said.

"It was so much fun," I say.

"Yeah," she says.

She stands, and I think maybe she's going to dig around in her closet where she used to keep her shoe box of Paper Things. That she'll want to build our world again.

Instead she just sort of stretches, then shakes her head. "God, we were such *dorks,*" she says.

I place my Paper Things back inside the folder, the folder back inside my backpack.

"Yeah," I say. "Dorks."

· 11 ·
AIRPLANES

Sasha has church on Sunday morning at ten, so Gage and Chloe come for me right after breakfast. Briggs is away until tomorrow, so they've had the studio all to themselves.

I feel a splash of warmth as we burst out the door of Sasha's apartment building onto the sidewalk. The sun is shining, the snow is melting. It's one of those end-of-March days in Maine that feel like a present — a little reminder that spring *is* here, even if the warm days won't really arrive (and stay) for about two more months. My Language Arts teacher would call this day "foreshadowing," I think—foreshadowing spring. Too bad I don't get extra credit for knowing that.

I reach down to pick up a penny, determined to make up for the fourteen cents I gave away on Friday.

"What are you going to buy with all that money?" asks Chloe, who knows about my daisy piggy bank at Briggs's.

"An apartment."

Chloe laughs.

"She's not kidding," says Gage, bending to pick up what we think is a nickel but turns out to be a souvenir coin of some sort. Neat but worthless. He chucks it aside.

"Not the rent," I clarify. "But once Gage gets a steady job and we find an apartment, I can help out with stuff like shampoo and toilet paper and toothpaste."

"Yeah, then you can stop using mine," Chloe says as she bumps shoulders with Gage. We both know she's kidding, but I still steal a glance at Gage's face to see if his pride's hurt. It looks like it would take a lot more than a little teasing today to bring my brother down.

When we get to the playground near Briggs's, I ask Gage if I can stay awhile. The place can be a treasure trove of dropped coins from adults chasing their kids on the old jungle gym or the rickety teeter-totter.

Gage looks around to see if there's any cause for concern. "All right," he tells me, "but be back at Briggs's in one hour."

Sasha and Linnie are always complaining about how easily I find money. They don't get how they miss it and I spot it every time. But it's not just the looking; it's *how* you look. When you first look down, you see everything—and nothing. It's as if your eyes can see only grayness. But if you tell yourself that there's treasure at your feet, your eyes will begin to see differences in the shades of gray: silvery cracks, charcoal pebbles, ashy litter. Then, when you find your first glimmering coin, your brain will understand exactly what you want, and it will start to find coins everywhere. It just takes patience.

So once I start finding coins under the benches, at the bottom of the slide, and all around the busted water fountain, I don't want to stop. I look at my watch and see that fifty minutes have gone by, but I tell myself, *Just one more.* Then: *OK, really one more.* And then: *Absolutely, positively just one more. Promise!*

I look at my watch again — holy moly, the whole hour has passed! I know I better hightail it back to Briggs's.

I race down the sidewalk, and I'm about a block away from the apartment building when I see the airplane man and Amelia, heading straight for me.

"Hi!" I say. Amelia wriggles happily as I approach. I reach out my hand and brush it over her from the top of her head, down her tickly back, to the fur right before her tail.

"Arianna, right?" the airplane man asks. I nod. "I have something for you," he says, and reaches into his coat. He pulls out a paper airplane. It's long and sleek and much more elaborately folded than I expected. He holds it between his thumb and fingers on one hand so I can get a better look. I don't think I've ever seen a paper airplane that appears so *real*.

"Wow, thanks!" I say. Then I realize that I don't actually know his name.

"Reggie," he says, seeming to read my mind.

"Thanks, Reggie," I say. The deep wrinkles around his eyes disappear as he smiles.

Just then something whizzes by us and ricochets off the side of the building, nearly hitting Amelia in the head. It's a chunk of brick — a big chunk.

"Get a job!" a guy about Gage's age yells as he walks past.

"Did he . . . did he just throw a *brick* at us?" I ask, shocked.

Reggie shakes his head slowly. "Not at us. At me." He leans down and holds Amelia's head in his hands, then looks in her eyes. "Wonder how so much hate grows in a person that young."

"I'm so sorry, Reggie," I say, kicking the brick into the gutter.

"No sense worrying yourself about it," he says, straightening back up. "I'm just glad you and Amelia didn't get hit."

I nod and give Amelia one last pat. "I've got to get going," I tell them. "But thanks again for the plane—it's terrific!"

Reggie gives a little salute, and I race back to the studio. I'm nearly there when I realize that I didn't even think to offer Reggie any of the change I'd collected today. Sure, I'd been searching extra hard to make up for the money I'd given him earlier this week, but the least I could have done was give him *some* of what I'd found today. After all, nobody was throwing bricks at my head and telling me to get a job.

And maybe it's because I'm so distracted thinking about the brick and Reggie and Amelia and my plane and the money I'd collected, but when I enter Briggs's apartment and see Janna standing there, I'm not startled.

"Hi," I say, my eyes hopping from Janna to Gage and back.

"There you are," she says, like we had an appointment or something. She has a scarf wrapped around her neck, and she's leaning against the counter with her arms folded. Gage is standing over some boxes on the floor, boxes she must have brought. Chloe is nowhere in sight.

"So your brother lets you walk around the city on your own, huh?" Janna asks, in her judge-y voice.

I frown. "I was just at the park around the corner. Then I ran into—"

"It's OK, Ari," Gage says. "I told Janna where you were and that you wouldn't be gone long."

Janna grunts and then looks around. "So, this is cute," she says, a sweep of her arm indicating the entire studio. "And the decorations are certainly . . . festive. But unless there's another room, I'm guessing you have to sleep here?" Her judge-y voice is back on, big time. "And where are all your things? Your boots and books and such," she says, frowning at my wet and ratty shoes.

And that's when it hits me: Janna thinks this is our place—mine and Gage's! I try to catch Gage's eye, to see if I'm supposed to play along, but he won't look at me.

"This is just temporary," Gage says. "Until we can find something better." Well, that's true, at least.

"Actually," says Janna, "I'm surprised you were

able to afford something in this building . . . in the West End. You must have been squirreling away money your entire senior year."

"We're subletting," says Gage quickly.

I watch Janna closely, wondering if she's buying this.

Janna nods and walks around slowly, examining the objects in the room. Most of it is Briggs's crazy party-supply stuff, but I notice that my Louisa May Alcott books are on the table, and my piggy bank has been taken down from on top of the cabinets and placed on the kitchen counter. I also notice that the place looks a lot cleaner than it usually does — no dishes in the sink or piled on the counter, no Cheerios or dust bunnies on the floor. Had Gage known that Janna was coming by?

"The decor is . . . interesting," Janna mutters, but the judge-y tone is gone. "And where do you hang your uniforms, Ari?"

I hear Gage's voice in my head: *Janna rule number one hundred twenty-four: Always hang up your school uniform.* I start to walk to the drawer under the TV set, where I stuff them (that is, when they're not stuffed in my backpack or at Chloe's), but Gage slides over to the closet.

"In here," he says. He opens the one closet in the studio, the one that holds all of Briggs's work pants and dress shirts, as well as the worn costumes he brings home from One Stop.

But when Gage opens the closet, only his clothes and my clothes are hanging there, including clean uniforms. When had Gage thought to do that?

"It works," Janna says, and turns to look at me. She reaches a hand toward my face but stops herself. "Your hair looks very pretty today."

I'd forgotten that it was in a gazillion French braids.

"You stayed at Sasha's last night," she says, her judge-y voice back. Janna used to hate it when Marianna would do up my hair or sew a little flower onto my clothes. She thought it was Marianna's way of telling Janna that she was a better mother.

"I wanted to give Gage and Chloe a date night," I say, which is partly true.

"Well," Janna says, pulling on her coat, "I'm glad you're doing so well." But she doesn't sound especially glad. "This should be everything," she says, nodding at the boxes on the floor.

"Janna—" I start before she makes it out the door.

She turns.

But I don't know what to say. "Thanks for bringing my stuff," I blurt lamely.

She nods and jets away.

· 12 ·
LUNCH SACKS

Ever since I can remember, I've had this theory that when each person is born, he or she is given an imaginary sack with the same number of happy moments, same number of horrible-news moments, same number of please-let-me-die-now embarrassments. So, while some people may have a bunch of bad moments all in a row, in the end, we'll all have experienced the same number of ups and down. We'll all be even.

Sasha tells me that that's a ridiculous way of thinking. "Think of people who are starving, or who live in countries where there is war, or whose parents are divorced," she says. "They suffer more."

But I like to think that even these people, whose hardships seem to come all at once, might get to experience the same number of joys in their lives as everyone else (and sometimes those feelings of joy pop up smack in the middle of hardship). And on the flip side, people whose lives seem perfect might also be suffering in ways we don't see, or might face hardships down the road.

But maybe Sasha is right. Maybe that is a ridiculous way of thinking. Yet sometimes, when it feels like all my troubles are piling up—Mama getting sick and dying, Janna and Gage fighting all the time, having to bounce from place to place with Gage and maybe missing out on the chance to go to Carter—it helps to think that there are only so many bad times in my sack. That sooner or later the good things will have to take over.

Anyway, this is what I'm thinking about as Sasha, Linnie, and I are going through the cashier line with our hot-lunch trays—that is, Sasha and I are carrying trays; Linnie brings her lunch to school, but she goes through the line with us 'cause she hates sitting alone—when the cashier stops me and says that I don't have any money left in my account. "Tell your mom, dear, that she forgot to send in this month's check."

Linnie leans over. "She doesn't have a—"

Sasha pulls Linnie toward our table to shut her up.

"Today I can give you an IOU," the cashier says, waving me through, "but don't forget it tomorrow."

"It's not like Janna to forget to send the payment," Sasha says when I join them. She sounds like Marianna.

Normally Sasha's comment would make me smile, but my head is cloudy. It's the second day of April.

Holy moly.

I sip slightly warm milk through a straw and wonder about my empty lunch account. Janna never forgets first-of-the-month responsibilities. (Rule number 28: Pay before play.) I always knew when it was a new month, because envelopes were on the counter, ready-to-be-mailed envelopes with checks inside—checks for bills, checks for school lunches and Girl Scout dues *(Am I no longer a Girl Scout?)*, checks for the newspaper delivery man and the Fresh Market next door that lets us say, "Charge it, please." No new balance means that she's no longer paying for my hot lunches.

Seeing Briggs's apartment must have convinced Janna that we're doing all right on our own. But we're not! Not really. Until Gage finds a real job, he can't afford to pay for my lunches. What am I supposed to do?

In the midst of my despair, another depressing thought hits me: April second. That would have made yesterday April Fools' Day. I feel the long tug of missing. Missing the days when everyone at Eastland Elementary marched through the school hallway wearing crazy hats. (Last year, Janna showed me a picture of my mother in elementary school wearing a handmade hat with wild pipe-cleaner shapes zinging out in all directions, and I made one just like it.) Missing the days when Gage would play April Fools' jokes on me. (One time he put salt in the sugar bowl and nearly fell over while he watched me take my first bite of oatmeal.) Missing the days when I didn't have to wonder where my next meal was coming from or where I was going to sleep each night or if Girl Scouts was no longer something I could put on my Carter application.

That's what I'm pondering when Linnie says, "GT prowl. Watch out!"

I look up and see Mademoiselle Barbary, our Gifted and Talented teacher, in the double doors of the cafeteria.

I lower my head and take a bite of my Tater Tots.

"She's coming," says Sasha.

I wish the approaching Mademoiselle were an April Fools' joke. When you're in kindergarten through third grade, being a GT kid is solid. You get to go to a special room and participate in projects, like making a time capsule or learning French. But when you're in fourth and fifth grade, it means getting pulled away from your friends at lunchtime to discuss "the unique problems of the gifted child." Lately it's been even worse because I've fallen into the category of "underachieving gifted child." Now I feel like she has her eyes on me all the time.

"What are your aspirations?" Linnie says, imitating Mademoiselle.

I can't help myself. I look up. That's when Mademoiselle gives me a little come-with-me wave. *Aaagh.* I say good-bye to my friends, pick up my tray, and follow her.

Seven of us sit around the big wooden table in Mademoiselle Barbary's room today: Daniel, Sam, Gracie, and I have been in this group since it started. She asks us if we are being appropriately challenged. "I am," shoots out Daniel, who is sitting next to me. We all nod, *We are, too!* (We learned last year that if you say that the work is too easy or that you're bored, you'll get tons more work to do — on top of the homework that the other kids get.)

I glance at the supplies on the shelves across the table. How I wish we could play with clay for a little while. "Invent something!" Mademoiselle Barbary used to say.

"Are you sure?" she says now. "I just looked over last quarter's grades, and some of you are not living up to your potential."

I look around the table, wondering if she's addressing anyone other than me.

"Often bright kids don't do as well as they could when the subject matter isn't interesting," she adds in her I-know-how-it-is voice.

Still no one speaks up. I start to feel sorry for her.

"Less than one quarter left, and we'll no longer be students at Eastland," Gracie offers. It's hard to say whether she's suggesting that our gifted problems won't matter much in a couple of months (after all, "everyone's *gifted* at Carter," as Sasha likes to say) or just stating a fact, but Mademoiselle is happy to run with it.

"How do you all *feel* about leaving Eastland?"

"I've started a bucket list," says Daniel.

"A bucket list?" Mason says. "The things you want to do before you *die*?"

"No. Not that. This is a list of things I want to do before I leave Eastland," says Daniel.

Mademoiselle presses her hands together like she's saying a prayer. "*Excellente!* Tell us one thing on your list."

Daniel pulls a small notebook the size of a passport out of his back pocket and thumbs through it.

There seem to be lots of lists and some sketches, too. He finds the page he was looking for. "'Talk to one person at Eastland that I've never spoken to.'"

"Magnifique," Mademoiselle says. She reaches for paper and suggests we each make a list and share them the next time we get together. Usually we come up with all sorts of excuses for not doing the extra tasks Mademoiselle assigns us, but for some reason, everyone seems really excited by the list idea— shouting out stuff they'd put on their list.

I lean over and ask Daniel if he's picked the person he'll talk to. He shakes his head and pushes his little notebook over so I can read the whole list.

1. *Talk to one person at Eastland that I've never spoken to.*
2. *Jump from the top of the bleachers into the pile of gym mats.*
3. *Free Gerald.*

I laugh after reading number 3. Everyone at Eastland knows about Ms. Finch's turtle, Gerald, even if they don't have Ms. Finch. She's had him forever, and he's grown so much that he almost doesn't fit in his tank. Everyone's just a little afraid of Gerald, even though he's not a snapper. Even Ms. Finch is afraid of him, which is why his tank is dirty all the time.

4. Cover the halls with paper snowflakes.

I realize that I'm not the only one missing the Eastland traditions. I grab Daniel's pencil and write "while wearing a crazy hat," after this item. He smiles.

I continue reading:

5. Get everyone to sing kindergarten songs in the cafeteria.
6. Skid from one end of the math hall to the other (after Mr. Grogan polishes the floor).
7.
8.

"How come seven and eight are blank?" I whisper. Mademoiselle glances at us. He points at the paper to keep me reading.

9. Be brave.

10. Persuade Arianna Hazard to do 1–9
 with me.

I look up and give him my you've-got-to-be kidding look.

He takes back his pencil and writes: *You can fill in seven and eight.*

"No way," I mouth.

Then he writes:

You might only go to four more schools in your whole lifetime. That's only four last days, ever.

I think about that for a moment. I reach for the pencil and write:

That's if I go to college.

He writes: *Of course you'll go to college.*

I force a smile, though what I'm thinking is that I might not if I don't get into Carter. *I'll think about it,* I write.

Daniel smiles and crosses off numbers 9 and 10.

· 13 ·
INVITATIONS

Gage picks me up from Head Start and calls Briggs.

"Hey, Brigster," he says. "What's up?" I know he's hoping that Briggs will tell us to come by tonight. While he talks, I travel in ever-widening circles on the sidewalk, looking for pennies.

The conversation drags on, but still no invitation. Gage tries harder: "So, do you have plans tonight?"

And then Gage's voice gets louder. "You're kidding! He can't do that, can he? Are you going to listen to him?

"All right," he says. "Yeah, sure, I understand."

"No studio tonight?" I say when he gets off the phone.

"Briggs's landlord says he's been violating the lease—that three people are living in the apartment instead of just one."

"But we're not living there!" Now I'm as mad as Gage.

"You and I know that, but tell it to the landlord."

"Does that mean we're never going back?" I want to ask him what we'll do about the stuff we left there—our clothes and the boxes from Janna—but now doesn't seem like the time.

"No," says Gage. He starts walking—to where, I don't know, but I follow. "It just means that we have to be a lot more scarce."

"Chloe's?" I ask hopefully when we get to the bus stop.

Gage shakes his head. "She has a friend from out of town staying with her tonight."

"Lighthouse?" I say, less hopefully.

"I hope not," says Gage, and boards the bus.

As it turns out, we're staying with Perry and Kristen. Gage met Perry down at the docks, and Kristen is his wife, even though they are hardly any older than Gage.

Right now we're sitting in their living room in South Port, which is not really in Port City. It's a whole different town, miles and miles from my school.

I try to decide where I should sit. There are two options: a big, nubby couch with an orange-and-green throw on it, and an easy chair. There's plenty of room on the couch next to Perry, but Kristen (who is in the other room and who probably looks pretty when she's happier) is none too pleased about having guests. So I'd hate to take any of her comfiness. I try to decide if she's more of an easy-chair person or a couch person. I can imagine her stretching out on the couch with one of her cats—I've counted three so far—the blanket covering her legs. But maybe she'd prefer the solitude of the easy chair, since she doesn't even seem to want to be near Perry right now.

I wish I could just go into the other room and do my schoolwork, but we're not the kind of overnight guests where the hosts announce, "Make yourself at home." We're practically strangers here. Gage sizes up the situation and grabs a metal chair from the kitchen table. He brings it into the living room and nods for me to sit on the couch next to Perry.

I sit on the far end of the couch, trying to make myself smaller, cuter, catlike.

Kristen comes into the room and takes the easy chair. I can't tell if she's mad about that or not.

Perry hands the remote to Gage, but Gage passes it off to Kristen and says, "We're happy to watch whatever you like."

Perry snorts. "Don't do that, man," he says, which seems to make Kristen even more annoyed. In fact, I kind of wonder if Perry brought us home just to aggravate Kristen.

Kristen tosses the remote back in Perry's lap.

When we walked in the back door, Kristen had been seated at the kitchen table. She pounced, expecting only Perry, wanting to know why he was late. Her face tightened when he introduced us (a look I recognized from Janna, who tried really hard not to look like an evil stepmother when we broke the forty-eight-hour rule and brought friends home unannounced) and said that we needed a place to crash tonight, that we'd thought we could move into our apartment today but it hadn't been ready after all. That's the sort of thing Gage tells people so they don't think we're homeless.

Which we're not, of course. We're just between homes.

"What about dinner?" Kristen had asked.

Perry had handed her the leftover pizza from Flatbread, where we'd gone after meeting up. Flatbread is a *très* big treat for us, and I thought Kristen might be pleased, but I guess she mostly felt left out. Anyway, it was a bad start to what was turning out to be a bad night.

Perry turns on a basketball game.

I stare at a spot on my blouse where I spilled tomato sauce. Since all of my extra shirts are at Briggs's, I'll have to wear this same top tomorrow. I don't dare ask Kristen and Perry if I can use their washing machine—I don't even know if they have one—but think maybe the stain will come out in the sink.

"May I use your bathroom?" I ask.

"Use the one upstairs," says Kristen. "It's cleaner."

On the way up the stairs, I grab my backpack. I lock the bathroom door and take my sweater and my blouse off. I turn on the water and wet the stain on my blouse. I look around for soap, but I can't find any. I look in the shower and see a small bottle of shampoo. It's green—I wonder if it will turn my white blouse green.

I decide to take the chance. It doesn't, but it doesn't exactly take the tomato sauce out either. It just sort of fades it. I put the blouse back on and button my sweater up over the wet spot. Maybe the stain'll fade even more once it's dry.

I'm on the landing, about to head back downstairs, when Kristen comes up the stairs.

"Do you want to sleep in the cupola?" she asks.

I look to my left and right. There is one bedroom on each side of the landing. One, with a big bed and men's clothes hanging over a chair, is clearly theirs. The other one has a twin bed, and I figure that's the guest room.

I point to the guest room. "Is that the cupola?"

"No, dummy," she says, but not in a mean way.

"Follow me." Using a metal rod that was resting against the wall, she opens a trapdoor in the ceiling, and a folding ladder comes down. I climb the ladder nervously. I definitely don't want to sleep in an attic, but I don't feel comfortable telling Kristen this. But when we get to the top, I see that it's not an attic at all. It's a tiny rooftop room with windows on all four sides—like the top of a lighthouse. There's a padded window seat all around that's wide enough to sleep on. The sun has set, but I can see streetlights and house lights below me.

"This was my grandmother's house," Kristen says. "I used to come and sleep up here all the time." She sits down on the edge of the seat. "Sometimes I still do."

"It's like being on top of the world," I say, looking over rooftops.

"My grandmother told me that before there were all these streetlights, you could see stars from up here." Then she looks at me. "It must be hard not having your own bed."

I shrug. "I'm OK as long as I'm with Gage," I say, and sit down beside her.

She nods. "He seems nice. Like the kind of guy who's considerate."

I want to tell her that as great as Gage is, sometimes we fight. But before I can say anything, she says, "Perry used to be really considerate."

That's when I realize that Kristen isn't mean; she's just sad—and maybe lonely. "Want to see something?" I say.

"Sure," she says in a polite voice. I think maybe she just doesn't want to head back downstairs yet.

I pull my Paper Things folder out of my backpack to show her. She clicks on an overhead light so she can see better.

"You've cut out lots of pretty things," she says, handling my Paper Things like they're made of tissue. "Imagine having a jewelry box like this one," she says, holding up the bureau with skinny little drawers.

"It's called an accessory tower," I tell her.

"I used to make beaded jewelry like the bracelet in this drawer."

"How come you stopped?"

Kristen shrugs. "Perry and I got married to be a

family. Then I lost the baby. I haven't been able to do much but think about it."

I don't know what to say, and so I do what every well-meaning person who tried to cheer me up after Mama died did: I say something stupid. "Maybe if you started making things again, you could buy one of these towers."

Kristen smiles. "Before the docks, Perry was learning woodworking. Maybe he'd build me one." She sighs and closes my folder. I wonder if I've made her sadder.

"Be sure to turn the light off before you get undressed," she says, standing up and walking toward the ladder. "There aren't any shades up here."

As Kristen creaks down the ladder, I pull out one of my Louisa May Alcott books. I find my place and read farther, taking a few notes in my notebook. I learn that Louisa May Alcott was poor, just like the characters in *Little Women*. She wrote that story to try to earn some money, to help her family out. I wish there were something I could do to help Gage and me—something other than collecting pennies, I mean.

I also learn that Louisa liked to keep lists. She wrote one about the bad habits she wanted to give up: "idleness, willfulness, impudence, pride, and love of cats." *Love of cats?* I wonder what Kristen would say about that. I wonder what *impudence* means. I wonder if I have it.

The list makes me think of Daniel's bucket list. I'm certainly not going to help him with it—even though I do like the idea of bringing back the snowflakes. But I think I understand what made him write it. As much as I'm looking forward to going to Carter—assuming I still have a shot at getting in—it's hard to imagine leaving Eastland Elementary.

I think back on the teachers I've had over the years, the classrooms that were mine. I think about upcoming graduation. Last year Mason and I got to be marshals at graduation—chosen because of our grades. That meant that I carried a baton and led the fifth-graders into the gym. The principal called each graduating student up to the podium after his or her name was announced, like Sasha's older brother:

William Sorotzkin, son of Alfonse and Marianna Sorotzkin.

Who will they announce for my parents? Mama and Dad, even though they're both dead? Janna, who I'm not even sure is still planning to come to graduation? Or will they just say *Arianna Hazard, sister of Gage Hazard*?

I close my notebook, and as I repack my backpack, I notice the paper airplane Reggie gave me the other day. I pull it out and examine it more closely. It's made of newspaper, and it has wings that look as graceful and as pretty as a bird's. Headlines fold in and out of the plane like ribbons with a secret code. I read the broken words to see if they create an interesting message, one for only me. They don't seem to, but I notice the word *Jiffy*, which gives me pause for some reason. What does this word *Jiffy* remind me of?

I unfold the jiffy wing, one crease at a time, making sure I remember how to put the plane back together again. Printed inside the wing is an ad for Jiffy Lube—and now I remember: Jiffy Lube was the name of the garage where Gage might be able to get a job!

Slowly, I trace the word *Jiffy* with my ink-smudged finger and then fold the airplane back up. Whether Reggie meant it or not, I can't help feeling that this really is a secret message.

I try to open the window. At first, it sticks, but I lean in, using my whole body to lift the frame. It pops open and lets the cool April air stream in. I hold the plane, this intricate gift made just for me, between my fingertips. I have so few things of my own. But I am thinking of wishes—wishes made on shooting stars, dandelion puffs, the flames of birthday candles. All those wishes floating off on the wind.

I close my eyes and imagine Gage telling me he got a job. I imagine our own apartment, with a room just for me. My own window, my own bed, a place for my Paper Things.

I look at that word on that wingtip one more time. Then I pull the plane back to my shoulder and let it fly.

Please, I whisper to the wind. *Please.*

NOTES

I'm sitting in Mr. O.'s Language Arts class, and I can hear Keisha talking with Sasha behind me. Keisha's one of the popular girls, and I can't remember the last time she talked to me or Sasha. Her voice is just loud enough for me to hear.

"Is Ari using some new product in her hair? Or is that . . . *grease?*"

I try hard to hear Sasha's response. Is she sticking up for me? But how can she? What can she say? She has no idea that I no longer have to pass the Janna test every single morning before heading out the door.

But this morning, Gage and I overslept, and I hardly had time to brush my hair before catching the bus back into Port City and all the way to Eastland. It seems like I have to wash it every day now to keep it clean. Plus, I had to throw on the same blouse that had the stain on it, so even though Mr. O.'s room is a furnace, I have my sweater buttoned up tight.

I tuck the greasiest strand of hair, the one that falls over my forehead, behind my ear and try to focus on my work. We're supposed to be writing book responses on books we've read on our own, our "independent reading" as Mr. O. calls it, and I'm writing mine on the Louisa May Alcott bio I was reading last night at Kristen and Perry's. I wonder if Mr. O. will think I'm cheating—making a book do double duty. But as much as I love to read, one book is all I've had time for lately.

"She smells, too," Linnie says from behind Keisha—Linnie, who can't resist being part of any conversation that Sasha's involved in.

Is she joking? I put my head down just a little lower, trying to smell my pits. She's not joking.

I stink. I curl over my desk, folding my arms in as close to my body as I can.

How could I help it? Gage's phone died, so we didn't have an alarm. We woke late, dressed, grabbed our things, and raced out the door. The bus stop was practically a whole mile away from where we slept last night. Gage kept screaming at me, "Hurry up, Ari! Run faster!" I was running as fast as I could, but my shoe has started to flap where the stitching is coming out, and it falls off easily. We made our first bus, but it was so crowded that Gage and I couldn't sit together. I had to sit next to a woman who kept sighing because she'd had two seats to herself and now she had to hold her things on her lap, and she didn't have much lap.

When we got to Congress Street, where our first bus route ended, Gage realized that we'd used up our bus passes. He'd have to go to an ATM to get more money to buy new ones.

"I can't wait here!" I shouted at Gage. "If I'm late again, I'll get detention."

"What are your choices, Ari?" Gage had snapped back.

"I'm running," I said. "We've run up to the East End plenty of times from here before."

"Then, go!" he'd yelled at me. Those were the last words we spoke to each other this morning.

So it's not much of a surprise that I don't look—or smell—my best today. But I can't very well explain the situation to Sasha and the others. My eyes start to tear, and I pinch myself on the thigh to give myself something else to focus on.

Mr. O. stops by Sasha's, Keisha's, and Linnie's desks. "Are you three reading the same book by any chance?" Mr. O. asks them. It's his way of telling them to get back to work. I'm glad. Maybe now Sasha knows what it feels like for your teacher to be disappointed in you—even though she still has three weeks left as a patrol leader.

I ignore Sasha and Linnie as much as I can all morning, which turns out not to be such a good idea. It seems to just make them higher-and-mightier. When the lunch bell rings, they're huddled together in front of Sasha's locker, whispering and shooting me looks. I can't tell if they're working up enough courage to tease me or if they're planning a hygiene intervention (the way Sasha and I once held an intervention to try to get Linnie to talk more softly— which, by the way, did not work). Either way, I'm smart enough to recognize a gang-up.

I'm also smart enough to devise a plan for avoiding them during lunch period.

While we were madly rushing around this morning, Kristen wrapped the leftover pizza in foil and stuffed it in my backpack. And even though I was hungry on the bus, I saved it. Since I don't have any money in my account anyway, and since I'd rather not be ambushed by Linnie and my supposed best friend, I figure I'll just skip the cafeteria altogether.

Instead, I ask Mr. O. for permission to stay in the classroom during lunch and work on my report. "You know I don't usually allow it," he says. "But I'll say yes today. You're going to need all the time you can get."

I gobble my pizza. When I dig deeper into my backpack to retrieve my notebook, I notice two things:

1. *An orange. A big, beautiful orange wedged between my binders.*
2. *A short note:* What's number seven and eight?

Daniel. I wonder if he's noticed that I'm not at my best today. I wonder if he cares that my hair is gross and I smell like the boys after a volleyball game. Maybe tonight we'll be at Chloe's and I can shower and send Gage to the Laundromat.

I think about Daniel's bucket list as I start to peel the orange. I can't seem to come up with anything I want to do one last time at Eastland before going to middle school, and I wonder what that says about me.

I think of other places I've left. If I'd known for longer than a day that I would be leaving Janna's, for example, what would I have wanted to do?

And just like that, I know: I would have crawled into the corner of the closet, smelled the cedar chips that Janna put in there to keep the moths away, and found the little stuffed hedgehog that everyone thought was one of my toys when they moved us out of Mama's apartment but really was a toy for Leroy, our dog. When we first went to live with Janna, I would take the comforter off my bed and drag it into the closet with me, along with the hedgehog. I liked sleeping in that small space, hidden away from everybody—from Janna, from the social worker, even from Gage.

I was in second grade when Mama died. Every day, Janna would bring me to school and leave me in the reading corner of Ms. Rich's classroom, where I'd curl up in a beanbag chair and read. Ms. Rich just let me stay there as long as I wanted. When I'd read every book in the reading center, she began to place books from the library near the beanbag. Eventually the books got longer, fatter, and juicier, until I was spending most of the day on that beanbag chair, lost in imaginary worlds. But then one Monday morning, Janna dropped me off, and instead of making my way to the reading center, I headed for my desk. I don't know what had changed, but somehow I felt ready to rejoin the class.

While I was adjusting to being back at school, the guidance counselor came to Ms. Rich's room once a week and brought me down to her office. She'd ask me questions about Mama and Gage, about living with Janna. She'd ask me how I was feeling and if I cried. I don't think I did cry much that year. (Maybe that's why I'm so leaky now.)

Inside the guidance office, there was a dollhouse. I longed to play with that dollhouse, to move the family members from room to room, discovering all the little treasures. It would be like a 3-D version of my Paper Things. But the counselor never said I could play with it, and I was always too afraid to ask.

I can feel a laugh rising through my body.

I pull out Daniel's note and write: *7. Sneak into the guidance office and play with the toys.*

And then I realize how foolish this would be — to say nothing of babyish. It's all fine and good to sneak around the school, doing things you're not supposed to if you're Daniel and you don't care if you go to Carter or not. (He has said as much in the presence of Mademoiselle Barbary many times.) But I do care. So I pull out a slip of paper and write:

Dear Daniel,

Thank you for the orange. It was delicious. I have given your proposal serious thought, and here is what I've concluded: I can't do all the items with you because the risk of getting caught is too high. But I have thought of two activities for numbers seven and eight, and if you'll do those, I'll do two of the other items with you. OK?

> *7. Help Arianna Hazard get a leadership role.*

> *8. Help Arianna Hazard apply to Carter.*

Ari

I pop the last bite of orange into my mouth and tuck the note into Daniel's desk.

· 15 ·
MAPS

Here is the greatest thing about Head Start: little kids don't care if your hair is greasy or if you smell a little bit (though I hope that the paper-towel-and-soap bath I gave myself between science and social studies helped with that). During circle time, four-year-old Omar will still leap into your folded lap. He will lean his head against your collarbone, so you can soak in the smell of his hair — not a baby-shampoo smell but a spicy cooking and hard-dreaming smell. He will trace his finger up and down your hand like a Hot Wheels on a racetrack, never noticing the dirtiness of your fingernails, the grime at your wrist caused by drying orange juice and lead pencil smudges. Or if he does, he won't care about these things. He will lean into you and pull your arms around him so that you feel like the best and most important person in the world.

Omar and I are wrapped up together, listening to Fran read about a gopher that wants his hat back, when West slips into the classroom to talk with Carol. I've never seen West at Head Start before, even though he was the one who told me that Carol and Fran needed a helper, and I can't help wondering if he's here because of me.

Sure enough, Carol comes over and tells me that West would like to speak with me. Omar is none too happy about this, but Carol offers to take my place and Omar grudgingly agrees.

"Hey, kiddo," West says, rubbing the stubble on his chin. Though he's older than Gage, West is still pretty young—younger than any of my teachers. At Lighthouse, the kids are always trying to get his attention, especially the girls. I pull my arms in closer, in case the paper-towel bath didn't do the trick.

"I haven't seen you and Gage lately," he says. "Everything OK?"

For some reason his question makes my lip tremble. I bite on it, hoping he didn't notice.

No such luck. "Come out here," he says gently, leading me into the front hall, where the kids' pussy willows lean down to listen.

I shouldn't have let on that anything's wrong. It's West, Gage says, who's keeping me out of the foster-care system, keeping the two of us together. He understands how hard Gage is working to find us an apartment, and he knows Gage is doing the best he can for me — for us.

"Things are OK," I say, trying to sound more optimistic — like Gage. "We've been staying with our friend Briggs." I don't mention Perry and Kristen or even Chloe. I want West to think we're fine.

"Yeah?" he says. "Where's that?"

"In the West End." I smile. West and West.

He gets it and smiles, too. "Must be good, then. How's Gage doing on the job hunt?"

"Hey, man!"

I look up. It's my brother. He's wearing his interview outfit: black pants, a clean white shirt, and a sport coat that Briggs has loaned him. He's clean shaven, too; when did he find the time to shower and change? And since when did he have an interview today?

"You're early!" I skip over to hang on his arm, happy to see him and relieved not to have to answer any more of West's questions.

"Aren't you looking dapper," West says.

"Just came from a job interview." Gage looks serious, and I start to squeeze his arm to console him, but suddenly he breaks into a grin. "I got it! I start at Jiffy Lube tomorrow morning."

I let out a little yelp of happiness and throw my arms around my big brother.

"Why didn't you tell me you were interviewing there today?" I ask, my voice muffled by his sport coat. "I would have spent every spare minute sending you good-luck vibes!"

"I didn't want you to get your hopes up, B'Neatie," he tells me, ruffling my dirty hair.

"I didn't know you were mechanically inclined," says West.

"Some. I used to own a car—a beater that I worked on all the time. But they train, too."

Gage's old car had been ugly as sin—covered in patches and four colors of paint. Janna had hated having it parked in front of the house, and I think she was hoping it would up and die one day. But Gage always managed to figure out what was wrong with it and find a way to make it work again.

I could still remember the day Janna took the car away. The night before, someone had called Janna and told her that Gage was one of the teenagers spotted at a house party across town. She'd been furious when she hung up the phone and had ordered me to get in her car, even though I was already in my pajamas. I got in the backseat and we drove around in the dark until we found the house—down a long dirt road—but we didn't go inside. Janna just took the tire iron out of her trunk and removed his back wheel.

I'd heard them arguing the next morning—it was what they call a knock-down, drag-out fight, their worst ever. Gage had had to walk home; he'd been the designated driver for the evening and had spent half the night scrambling to find replacement rides for his friends who'd been drinking. But Janna didn't focus on how responsible Gage had been; instead, she screamed at him for attending a party with alcohol in the first place and for letting his friends get drunk. "You're just like your father!" she'd shouted, making it sound like the worst insult ever.

Gage had said some pretty nasty things back at that point, which was when Janna called Joe's Salvage and had them tow his car away. Even if Gage could have figured out where she'd stashed the missing tire, he didn't have the money to get it out of impound, so that was the end of Gage's ugly car.

But now Gage will be working on *lots* of cars, and maybe he can even save up enough money to buy one of his own—not to mention he can now afford to pay rent! We will finally have our own apartment—our own beds *and* our own shower! Sasha, Linnie, and Keisha won't have any reason to gossip about me then.

When I go to say good-bye to Omar and the others, I feel like I'm walking on air. How funny to think that a day that started off so terrible could turn into one of the best days ever.

16

CONFETTI

One hot shower later, I'm sitting at the bar in Chloe's kitchen with her and Nate. The song "All You Need Is Love" is blasting from Nate's iPad, and a bouquet of sunshiny-yellow daffodils is sipping water from a clean spaghetti-sauce jar in front of us—Gage brought them for Chloe. Tonight we're celebrating.

Gage is frying up pork chops and applesauce, which I haven't had since we left Janna's. He bought the pork chops and all the fixings to go with them, too: baby potatoes, broccoli with cheddar-cheese sauce, and sparkling cider! When the chorus of the song comes around, we all sing loudly. It might be true that the only thing we need is love—but a pork-chop dinner and a job at Jiffy Lube sure don't hurt!

"To Gage's new job!" Chloe says, and we clink mismatched glasses. My glass has a picture of Charlie Brown and a kite. Gage's has a picture of a sailing ship. But my eyes rest on Nate's glass, which has a picture of an airplane.

"It was the plane!" I say suddenly, remembering the wish I made on Reggie's paper airplane with its *Jiffy* wing.

"What plane?" Chloe asks, and I explain about the airplane that Reggie made for me and how one of its wings hid an advertisement for Jiffy Lube.

"I made a wish and sailed the plane out the window at Perry and Kristen's," I tell Gage. "And what I wished for was that you'd get a job at Jiffy Lube—and you did! And I didn't even know that you had an interview!"

"That sounds like one lucky plane," Chloe says, her voice impressed.

"What are you talking about? It was my superior mechanical knowledge that got me the job!" Gage shouts from the stove.

Nate turns down the music and props his iPad up on the bar so that we can look at ads for apartments.

"Look for places in the East End," Gage says. "It's a lot closer to Carter."

I force myself to smile. I love that Gage is so confident that I'll get into Carter, but he doesn't know about all the late homework assignments or the disappointed looks from the teachers. I'm not even sure he remembers that I haven't been given a leadership role yet—and time is running out.

"To Carter," Nate says, and raises his glass. I raise my Charlie Brown glass along with everyone else and we clink glasses again. I stuff my concerns deep down; I don't want to ruin the celebration.

"How much rent can you afford?" asks Nate.

Gage tells him, and Chloe says that it will be hard to find a two-bedroom for that price.

"It'd be a lot easier to swing if there were two of us pitching in for rent," Gage says. At first I think he's talking about me, and I cringe; how the heck am I supposed to find enough discarded change to pay half the rent? But then I notice that he's looking at Chloe—and he's got a big, teasing grin on his face.

Chloe's face turns the color of her red hair. "Not until we make the one-year mark," she says. But she's smiling, too, and I can tell she's glad that he asked, even if it was mostly a joke.

I look down at the iPad, feeling relieved. As much as I love Chloe, lately I've been looking forward to me and Gage having a place all our own—at least for a little while. "We can get a one-bedroom and I'll sleep on the couch," I say, glancing up again. But then it occurs to me that we don't have a couch. We don't have any furniture. I wonder if Gage's job will pay him enough for us to get some.

Chloe takes over the iPad and finds a listing for a one-bedroom in the East End that's only a little more than we can afford. She reads, "A charming place with a lot of potential!"

"Boy, there are some red flags," says Nate. "'Charming' means small. And 'potential' means it's probably gnarly."

"I don't mind cleaning!" I say, and lean over to get a better look.

Gage comes over to see, too. "It's tiny," he says. "Hardly bigger than Briggs's studio."

It *is* a little small-looking. And it could do with a good, hard scrubbing. But, still—our own place in the East End! "We can do tiny."

Nate scoffs. "You couldn't even spread out your paper dolls in an apartment that small."

"We'd have to be the size of Miles," says Gage, "to fit in that apartment."

Chloe looks confused, so I tell her that Miles is my oldest cutout, and Gage tells her that Briggs accidentally ripped him and now he has tape across his chest.

Nate finds a listing for an apartment in the West End that has only one bedroom, but it has a little office that could be my bedroom. "Applicants must have two years of good recent landlord references," he reads.

I frown at the screen. "You mean, you already have to have had an apartment for two years?"

Gage nods. "I would like to rent this apartment," he says in a fake deep voice.

It's the game! "Do you have references?" I ask in my fake-lady voice.

"How do you get references?" he says.

"By renting an apartment," I say.

"I would like to rent *this* apartment."

"Do you have any references?"

"How do you get references?"

"By renting an —"

"All right, all right," says Nate. "Anyway, it says here that you can have a cosigner if you don't have references."

"What's that?" I ask, wobbling back onto my stool.

"Someone who has a record of being financially responsible," Gage says.

"Maybe Janna would cosign for the apartment," Chloe says before taking another sip of cider.

I raise my eyes at Gage. Would we really visit Janna? Ask her to help us? My heart stumbles, gives an extra beat. I wonder what she's doing right now. For some reason I picture her slicing onions, chopping them into little tiny chunks.

But Gage is shaking his head. "It's not an option" is all he says. "Besides, it's in the West End, and Carter is in the East." He turns off the fire under the pots and pans. "Someone set the table," he says, by which he means the bar. Nate turns to grab some plates, while Chloe shrugs and goes back to looking.

"Here's one in the East End," Chloe says. "It's a two-bedroom, and it has laundry in the building."

"What's it look like?" Gage asks.

"It looks OK," Chloe says. "It says 'prospective tenant must income qualify.'"

"What does that mean?" I ask, getting as close to the pictures on the screen as I can. The kitchen has wooden cabinets and an orange countertop. There's gray carpeting on the floor. The bathroom has a shower stall. It looks a little dated but much cleaner than the other place. And it has two bedrooms! I wonder if I can paint the walls of my bedroom turquoise. In the latest Pottery Barn catalog, a lot of the rooms were turquoise.

"It probably means that you can't make over a

certain income. You should call," Chloe says, grabbing his phone from the coffee table.

Gage places two platters on the bar. The pork chops, with brown bits mixed into the applesauce, look amazing. So does the broccoli with cheese. He brings over a large bowlful of steaming baby potatoes and takes his place on a stool.

"Call about the apartment," says Chloe, holding out the phone.

"I'll call," says Gage, scooping up pork chops and sliding them onto our plates.

Chloe sings, "It's in the East End. It could be gone tomorrow." She is still holding his phone.

I've cut my first piece, and my mouth is watering. I can already taste the juiciness of the pork chop. As much as I want Gage to call about the apartment, I want Chloe to put the phone down and pick up her fork even more.

The Beatles sing "Let It Be." I wonder if Nate chose the song or if it's a coincidence.

Gage stares at Chloe.

She stares back.

Nate gives me a grimace that says *awkward*.

Gage rests his forearms on the table and sighs. "I can't call, Chloe," he says. "Janna cut my phone service today."

She throws the phone down on the counter. "You've got to be kid—"

Gage interrupts. "Please don't, Chloe," he says. "Tonight, *please*, let's not let Janna ruin this celebration."

Chloe pauses. You can tell that she doesn't want to change the subject. Maybe she wants to rail about Janna; maybe she wants to offer him her phone. But she stops herself, picks up her fork, and shrugs.

Ever notice that a shrug hardly ever means what it's meant to?

17

REPORTS

I wait by my locker for Sasha to finish her duties as patrol leader. Every morning since fifth grade started, we've met here. I've decided that today will be the day I tell her everything. I'll tell her about leaving Janna's, Gage's new job, and the Jiffy Lube airplane. I'm looking forward to having things back to normal between us.

But she doesn't come. It isn't until Mr. O. pops his head outside his door and tells anyone who is still standing in the hall to come on in that I go to get my social studies book and find the note from her inside my locker. It reads: *Thanks for calling me back last night. AGAIN!* Then there is someone else's handwriting—Linnie's, I'm pretty sure—right below Sasha's: *Do you know you're the only fifth-grader who still doesn't own a cell phone?*

I grab my book and slam my locker closed. So Sasha has called Janna's after all—and more than once. But obviously Janna hasn't told her that I don't live there. What does Janna say instead? That I'm eating dinner? Busy? Gone somewhere? Whatever the excuse, Sasha clearly thinks I'm ignoring her.

As for Linnie's remark, that isn't even close to being true. Loads of kids at our school don't have cell phones. Last I knew, Sasha didn't have one either—though I wonder if she just got one and that's why she was calling.

That, or she still wants to talk about my appearance.

I can't find out which, because she and Linnie, who are already at their seats in homeroom, pretend they don't see me when I walk in. I'm about to say something, to tell Sasha that I have something very important to tell her—something that will explain everything—when Daniel grabs my backpack and yanks.

"Cut it—"

"I'll do it," he says.

"You'll do what?"

"Help you get a leadership role. And apply to Carter."

I had forgotten all about my note to Daniel. I want to ask Daniel how he plans to help, but just then, the morning announcements begin. While we stand for the national anthem, I look over at Sasha. We always exchange a glance during the anthem, our here-we-go-again look. But today she doesn't turn back, doesn't catch my eye. She looks at Linnie instead.

It's OK, Arianna Hazard, I tell myself. *You like being invisible. You're good at it.* I decide not to tell Sasha about my situation, after all—not until she acknowledges that I exist.

All morning long, I glide in and out of classes, pretending that I'm a ghost. It's actually amazing how easy this is. Most of my teachers have long given up calling on me, which normally would upset me but which I don't mind today. It just makes being invisible all the easier.

At lunchtime, I ask Mr. O. if I can do work in his room again. He asks to see the work I did yesterday during lunch. Fortunately, I've completed the introduction and three new pages. I've written about Louisa May's childhood—how she'd had to move frequently and how she'd written in her journal, "I wish I was rich, I was good, and we were all a happy family this day."

"Very good, Arianna," Mr. O. says, handing my pages back to me. "Let's see if you can't match yesterday's productivity. I'll be in the teachers' lounge if you need me."

Inside my backpack I have a salami-and-cheese sandwich that Nate made me. Now that Gage has a job, I told him after breakfast that Janna had not only stopped paying for his phone but also my hot lunch—though I wish I hadn't, since Gage's whole body tensed as he sprayed angry words: "Why didn't you tell me, Ari! I can't believe she cut you off! I just assumed that you were set for the rest of the year!"

Chloe went over and put her arm around him, but he was too mad to be comforted by her touch.

"She just wants to put the screws to us," he

continued. "Like always, Janna has to prove that she's the one who knows everything. I can't believe she would do that to you, Ari!"

"Ari probably qualifies for free lunch," Nate said.

"Not until we can put an address on the form," Gage replied.

I probably could have started the circle game with that line, but I knew Gage wasn't in the mood to play.

He sat down on the couch beside me and held open my backpack while I tried to fit in some clean clothes and my schoolwork, too. "I promise I'm going to fix this," he said.

I struggled to slip my Paper Things folder into my backpack.

"Do you believe me, Ari?"

I looked at Gage and nodded.

"We can do this. I know we can. We're a team, right?"

"A team," I said.

I'm writing the next section of my report when Daniel walks into the room.

"Did you get permission to be here?" I ask. I'm afraid that he's going to get us both in trouble.

"Which items on my list do you want to do?" he asks, ignoring me and flipping a chair around so he's straddling it backward.

"There's one more round of leadership announcements before the end of the year," I say. "Can you guarantee that one of those jobs will be mine?"

He shakes his head. "Face it, Ari. The odds of getting one of those final positions are slim."

I look away for a moment, wondering if everyone in the school has noticed how badly I'm doing.

"But," he continues, "I can give you a *suggestion*."

I raise my eyebrows.

"Invent your own leadership role," Daniel says.

I frown. "What do you mean?"

"Come up with something helpful to do and then ask a teacher if you can do it. I bet you'd even get extra credit for having come up with the role yourself!"

Extra credit sounds good. I can use all the credit I can get. "I volunteer at Head Start," I say. "Do you think that would count?"

Daniel makes a face to show that he's thinking, but I can tell he's not especially impressed. "Lots of kids volunteer," he says. "I think you need something else, something that really sets you apart. Though having volunteer work on your application can't hurt," he adds, likely noticing my sadness.

"OK," I say slowly. "So, what sorts of helpful tasks could I volunteer to do?"

"I don't know," Daniel admits. "But there must be something that needs doing here at Eastland— something besides safety patrol and tutoring math."

I shrug. "Yeah, maybe," I say, when what I really want to say is *Thanks for nothing.*

"So, which of the items on my list do you want to do?" he asks again, opening his little book.

"None," I say. "You didn't get me a leadership role."

"True," he says. "But all you've got to do now is come up with an idea, and you'll have a leadership role to put on your application. So, which one should I put off till you're ready?"

I can't help myself. I look at his list. I'm definitely not going to sneak into Ms. Finch's room again, no matter what I think of poor Gerald. And I'm not sliding down the math hallway either.

I consider making snowflakes. I'd missed making them back in November when we had the first snowfall, even more than I expected. I'd been in Mr. O.'s room, studying the American Revolution, when Linnie announced that the first flakes were falling. We'd all cheered and started putting our textbooks away in anticipation of paper and scissors. But Mr. O. had sighed and said, "Not this year." We just kept on reading about Paul Revere as if nothing exciting were happening right outside our very own window, as if the traditions of the Eastland Tigers—traditions that my mom and dad and Janna and Gage had all participated in—had never even existed.

That's when a tiny little idea rests on me, like a fluffy six-pointed snowflake that has to be examined quickly before it melts away.

"A traditions club," I whisper.

Daniel leans in. "What?"

"I could start a club for the kids who still want to do the Eastland traditions."

"Like snowflakes and crazy hats?"

I nod. "And maybe even the fifth-grade campout!"

Daniel looks unconvinced. "That would be cool. But you'd have to follow the procedures for establishing a club: presenting the administration with the club's mission statement; conducting a student survey to see how many kids want to join; finding a chaperone; requesting a room; sending home permission slips. It's a lot of work," he cautions.

I'd forgotten that Daniel had tried to establish a robotics club last year. And if Daniel couldn't get kids to stay after school for robots, I'm pretty sure I'm not going to get them to give up their free time for snowflakes. Besides, half the fun of the Eastland traditions was breaking up the boring school-day routine.

"This is useless," I say, dropping my head to my desk. "It's too late to get a leadership role; there's not enough interest in starting a club. . . . Let's face it: I'm not going to have anything impressive to put on my application to Carter. I don't know why I'm even bothering to apply."

Daniel is quiet for a minute. "Maybe you could start a campaign to get the Eastland traditions back—get them back for everyone," he says.

I look up. "A campaign?"

"Yeah, you know, like those kids who campaigned to get the street out front renamed in honor of Ms. Taber." Ms. Taber used to be our school librarian. "You could put up posters, get kids to sign a petition. . . . I'll help. Give me your number."

"I don't know. . . . A club suggests that you're adding something to a school. A campaign sounds like you're challenging the rules. I don't want Carter to think I'm a troublemaker."

"Better than Carter not thinking of you at all," Daniel says.

He has a point. I scribble Gage's cell phone number on a slip of paper and pass it to Daniel.

It's not till after the bell rings that I remember that Gage's phone number no longer works.

· 18 ·
BUS PASSES

Since I spent most of my lunch period talking with Daniel, I didn't get much farther on my biography. What will my final term progress report—the one I have to attach to the application to Carter—look like? I'm going to have to work *très, très* hard to bring my grades up—which hopefully will be easier once Gage and I move into our new apartment.

But Daniel's suggestion has been spinning around in my mind since lunch, and I am more determined than ever to do what I need to get into Carter. Maybe it won't be enough, but at least I won't have gone down without a fight.

So as soon as the last bell rings, I head to the office and request an application.

I expect Mrs. Benoit, the secretary, to ask me why Janna isn't the one picking up the application, and I've got a lie all ready to go, but she just smiles and hands over the form as though kids ask for applications to Carter all the time.

As I walk out of the office, I hear a voice calling my name.

It's Ms. Finch, standing by the bench in the front hall. "Ari," she says. "Everything OK?"

I pause, wondering what she means, and then I realize: she thinks I've just come from the principal's office. Because in her eyes, I am no longer Arianna Hazard, star pupil. Instead, I'm Arianna Hazard, the girl who did Mr. O.'s assignment during computer lab, who is often late and disorganized, and whose hair looks like it hasn't seen a brush in a month.

I feel pressure behind my eyeballs and blink furiously. I will not cry in front of Ms. Finch. "Everything's good," I say as brightly as I can manage. I want to tell her that things will be better from now on—that Gage and I are on our own now and that we've been struggling, but Gage has a full-time job and soon we'll be getting an apartment, which means no more tardies and no more doing my homework during computer lab. But I don't dare. Not just because Gage told me not to, but because I'm not going to do one more thing to jeopardize my application to Carter. I'm pretty sure they're not looking for a kid who's homeless. (Which I'm not, of course. I'm just a temporary . . . What does Briggs call me? *Floor surfer.*)

"I'm on my way to Head Start," I offer instead. "I volunteer there in the afternoons."

Ms. Finch raises her eyebrows, like she's surprised. Another reminder of just how far I've fallen in her estimation. Like Daniel said, lots of kids in fifth grade volunteer. It's so they can say on their middle-school applications that they've done service learning. "Maybe one day you can come by my room and tell me more about it," she says. "I'd like to hear."

I nod, not sure what to make of that. Is it possible

that she doesn't believe me—that she thinks I'm making up an after-school activity just to look good?

Has it really come to that?

I'm sitting at the cutting table at Head Start. Juju is next to me, cutting a shiny stove from a Home Depot flyer. Omar is tearing paper in his usual way. A couple of other kids have gravitated to us today as well. There's a page in the catalog I'm flipping through that says, "May Day's Coming!" and it has people dressed in white, playing games like croquet, ringtoss, and horseshoes. I've only played games like that once. Back in third grade, this girl Tori, who Sasha and I were friends with before she moved to Buffalo, invited us to her eighth birthday party, which was at her grandmother's house in Falmouth. We took turns playing lawn games— though none of us wore white. I remember how Tori's dad had coached her from the sidelines, telling her how to hold the horseshoe, how to take aim, how to throw it high enough and far enough that it circled and landed around the stake. I wondered at the time if my dad would have taught me how to play horseshoes in our little backyard if he hadn't died in Afghanistan. I cut out the horseshoes for my paper dad.

After that, I don't feel like cutting out Paper Things. Instead, I pick up a catalog page that Omar has discarded, fold it, and cut out a snowflake. It's small but complicated, with a little star in the middle. I picture the halls of our school covered in snowflakes, and that gives me an idea. What if my campaign started invisibly? What if Daniel and I secretly hung snowflakes all around the school like some sort of spring blizzard to bring attention to the lost traditions?

I think about enlisting Sasha, but I know that at this stage, I could never persuade her. First of all, she thinks Daniel is weird. Second of all, she has a leadership role and wouldn't want to jeopardize it by sneaking around after hours and bending school rules. Third, she still isn't talking to me. Fourth, she thinks Daniel is weird.

But what if the spring blizzard isn't enough to get

kids—and administrators—excited about bringing back the traditions? Or worse, what if no one gets it? Maybe we need something else, something to make our mission perfectly clear.

The ideas are percolating as I grab another catalog page and start cutting. If the snowflakes got some kids' attention, we could maybe get them to fight for our cause. They could help us stage an impromptu Crazy Hat Day. We'd have to come up with a way of spreading the word and finding kids who'd be willing to risk getting in a bit of trouble by wearing a hat to school. But once everyone saw the great hats—hats like the upside-down ice-cream cone that Briggs bought me—surely excitement would spread for all the other great Eastland Elementary traditions.

"Ari, what are you *doing*?" asks Juju, pushing a catalog closer to me. She's clearly disappointed in my choice at the cutting table today.

"I'm making a snowflake, see?" I unfold my triangle to show her the lacy shape I've cut.

"Snowflakes?" Carol says as she passes by us. "It's April, Ari! We don't want snowflakes now. We want warm spring weather!"

I smile and tell Carol about my campaign to bring back the Eastland Elementary traditions, starting with a surprise spring blizzard."

"What a great idea!" Carol says. She brings me white paper.

Fran pulls up a chair next to me. "I've never made a paper snowflake," she says. "Have you guys?" she asks the group of Starters at the cutting table. They shake their heads. "Would you show us how?"

She's surprisingly fast with scissors. In no time at all, she's cutting really complicated snowflakes. The little kids' snowflakes are a lot simpler—random shapes cut out of pieces of paper folded just in half—since it's too hard for them to cut through multiple layers of folded paper. Soon they're bored by the assignment and start to get restless.

"I know," says Fran, and she goes and gets glue bottles and glitter. "Let's make our snowflakes sparkle!"

This the kids know how to do! They squeeze glue onto the snowflakes, shake glitter on top of the glue, and then slide the excess glitter off into a tub. Later, Fran or Carol will ask me to refill the shaker bottles with the glitter from the tub; they both hate that job. "You have glitter in your hair and underneath your fingernails for a week," says Carol. But I don't mind. I like the sparkles.

At one point, Fran tears a page from a catalog, but she doesn't fold it into a snowflake. Instead she sets the page to the side.

I look more closely. It's a page of bikes.

"I'm hoping to buy a bicycle this spring," she says when she notices me looking. "To ride to work. But they're much more expensive than I imagined."

I nod. The past two months have shown me just how expensive things are. Once again, I am so, so grateful that Gage now has a job. I can still barely believe how lucky —

"Hey!" I say. "I think I might know a way to help you get a bike!" I tell her about Reggie and the wishing plane.

"Did he know that your brother was applying for a job at Jiffy Lube?" Fran asks.

"No! *I* didn't even know! Reggie just happened to give me a plane that had the ad. I made a wish and flew the plane out a window."

Fran is quiet as she cuts a six-pointed flake.

"I could take that catalog page to Reggie . . ." I offer.

Fran laughs at my persistence. "Why not?" she says. "Wishing never hurt." She slides the picture over to me, and I walk into the hall to carefully place it and the snowflakes in my backpack.

"Wait—" Fran joins me in the hall with her purse. She takes three dollar bills from her wallet and hands them to me. "Would you give him this from me, for his time—and his talent?"

"I don't think you have to pay him," I say. "He makes free airplanes for kids all the time."

"I know," she says. "But it seems like the right thing to do."

I wonder what Reggie will think of my request. Will he mind that I'm asking him for another plane—this time for someone else? And what will he think when I tell him that his paper airplane made my wish come true?

· 19 ·
RECEIPTS

After the good-bye song, Fran races off to an appointment. Clusters of parents arrive to pick up the Starters, until only Carol and I are left. This is really unusual. Gage typically picks me up in the middle of dismissal, not at the end. "Why don't you call Gage, see how close he is?" Carol suggests, handing me her phone.

I start to dial Gage's number but quickly realize that it won't do any good. "I can't," I say. "Gage doesn't have his phone today."

"No phone?" I can tell that this frustrates Carol. I can also tell that she is eager to leave. She has to pick her baby girl up at day care.

"It's OK," I say. "Gage will be here soon."

"I can't leave you—"

"If Gage doesn't come in fifteen minutes," I say, "I'll go to Lighthouse and tell West." I won't, though. I know that West has looked the other way before, but that's because he really believes Gage is doing what's best for me. If I show up at Lighthouse complaining that Gage never picked me up, I don't know if West would be able to keep that one to himself.

Instead I'll go to Chloe's. Surely Gage would think to look for me there.

Carol is still uncertain.

"The bus stop is only two blocks away," I say. "And it will be light for another hour or so."

"All right," she says. She takes a receipt out of her purse and writes her number on it. "Call me when you're with Gage."

Carol keeps looking back as she walks down the street to her car. We both want Gage to show up before she's gone.

I don't know whether I'm more mad at Gage or afraid for him. What if something happened during his training at Jiffy Lube? I don't know a whole lot about mechanic shops, but they seem like the kind of place where accidents could happen. Maybe Gage was distracted because of what I'd told him this morning about Janna no longer buying my school lunch. Maybe he'd been thinking about that instead of focusing on what he was doing and—

I force myself to stop thinking like that. He's probably fine. Maybe he just lost track of time, or maybe his training went on longer than expected.

I wait around for what feels like about fifteen more minutes, and then I head to the bus stop. I see the bus coming as I approach, and I race the last block and catch it just in time.

The bus going into town isn't crowded at this hour, since most people are leaving their jobs in the city and heading for their homes in the suburbs, so I have no trouble finding a seat all to myself. But now that I'm actually on the bus, I'm plagued by a new set of worries: What if Gage arrived at Head Start right after I left? Would he be mad at me for leaving? Would he think to look for me at Chloe's? Should I have left him a note somehow, maybe tucked in the door to the Head Start building, letting him know where to find me?

I try to put myself in Gage's shoes. If I were Gage and I showed up at Head Start late and saw that my little sister was missing, who's the first person I would go to for help finding her? It would definitely be Chloe, I assure myself. She'd keep a level head and would know just what to do.

The bus pulls up to the stop by Chloe's place. I get off and start trudging up the hill. Maybe I'll even bump into Gage as I'm walking!

Rather than keeping my head down and looking for pennies, I scan the faces that I pass, hoping to spot Gage. There's a woman covered in blankets, leaning against the wall of a building. A man with dreadlocks who is shouting loudly, though no one appears to be listening. A bearded man who walks toward me with his hands out. I offer a smile — friendly but not *too* friendly — and walk faster.

The door to Chloe's apartment building feels like home. I push it open and climb the stairs, trying not to notice the smell of pee.

I knock on the door, ready to reassure Chloe

when she sees me standing here without Gage. But even after three knocks, no one answers. It hadn't occurred to me that Chloe or her roommates might not be home. I turn the doorknob to see if the door is unlocked, but no such luck.

Now what? Should I wait here for Chloe or one of her roommates to show up—or for Gage to show up, knowing this is where I'd most likely be? But if Gage knows that Chloe isn't home right now, would he assume I'd know that, too? In that case, where would he think to look for me?

Briggs's studio.

I dash down the stairs. What if he's already there? Will he leave as soon as he sees that I'm not there? *Then* where will he look for me? How the heck are we supposed to find each other when neither of us has a phone?

Holy moly, Gage must be as worried about me right now as I am about him. I fly back down the hill toward the stop for the bus going to the East End.

The bus stop is spilling over with adults waiting to take the bus out of the city, back to their homes with their bright kitchens and their shiny granite countertops and stainless-steel appliances. I picture them eating with their families at long tables, tables filled with platters of food. Afterward, they'll help their kids with their homework and the kids will grumble, but they'll also be glad because they won't be scared or embarrassed when the teacher comes around to collect their work.

Even though lots of people are loaded down with briefcases or shopping bags, no one is sitting down at the bus stop. I peer past the crowd and into the bus shelter; a man is curled up on the bench with his back turned toward the crowd. Every so often someone shoots him a grumpy look, and a woman next to me mutters, "Lousy drunk."

I take a closer look at the man. He seems familiar to me. Do I know him from the soup kitchen?

Just then, the man turns over on his back, and suddenly I know exactly who he is. And I know for sure that he's not drunk, just tired. Bone tired. The kind of tired that comes after a long day of training at Jiffy Lube and pulls you down, even though you're supposed to be picking up your little sister from Head Start.

The man sleeping on the bench is Gage.

The bus pulls up, and I wait until all of the people have boarded before I shake my brother awake.

Gage is even more distressed than I expected him to be — but not for the reason I expected.

He looks at his watch. "Shoot, shoot, shoot!" he says, only he doesn't say *shoot*. "We've got to go! Hurry up!" He looks frantic.

At first I think he's still half asleep, convinced we've overslept for work and school. But when I start to explain that it's late afternoon, he interrupts me.

"I know that, Ari. But we have to be across town in ten minutes!"

"What for?" I ask, rushing to keep up with his long strides. I wonder if we'll be crashing with someone new tonight — a friend from Jiffy Lube, maybe. At least it's not Lighthouse.

"To see the apartment!"

I stop. "What?"

"The two-bedroom apartment. I called this morning from work," Gage yells over his shoulder.

He's still hurrying along and is already crossing Maple Street. "Let's go!"

I run to catch up with him. "We're going to see an apartment?"

"Not if you don't hurry. The landlord said he'd meet us at five. I don't know how long he'll wait."

I'm practically skipping as we make our way to the bus headed to the East End. I decide not to remind Gage that I was waiting for him in the East End. He still hasn't put two and two together and realized that he forgot to pick me up from Head Start. And maybe, just maybe, if everything goes right tonight, he'll be too distracted by happiness to remember.

· 20 ·
VOUCHERS

It's weird how something from when you were little will pop back up again later in life. I remember being in the car—it must have been with Janna, since Mama didn't drive—stopped at a light and looking out the window at a row of houses, all connected. Each house had its own tiny fenced-in backyard. There wasn't much grass in each yard; it was mostly dirt that had been dug up by plastic shovels, bent spoons, or paws. Some of the yards had little hibachi grills, and most were scattered with plastic toys— toppled Big Wheels and baby dolls lying facedown in the dirt.

"I'd like to live there," I'd said.

"In public housing?" Gage had asked.

"It looks like fun," I'd said. "Everyone's together."

It's those very same houses that we're coming up to now. The houses aren't in the part of the East End where Janna lives (outside loop with views of the harbor) or where Sasha lives (tiny inside streets near the shops). Instead, they're down near the warehouses. Warehouses that used to be factories, according to Gage, but now just store stuff.

"Remember when I used to want to live here?" I ask my brother, now that I've caught up.

He's looking at a slip of paper. "We're not in these units," he says. "We're across the street."

I look up at a gray building that looks less like apartments and more like offices for the warehouses. It has a flat roof and rectangular windows.

Gage and I have just gone in through the glass front door and are trying to make sense of the numbers on the mailboxes when an older man comes up the steps behind us.

"Gage?" he asks.

It's the landlord. Gage shakes his hand, introduces me, and apologizes for being late.

"Not to worry," the man says. "These things happen." He leads us back outside and around the corner of the building. "The apartment has its own entrance," he says as we follow him down a small stairway. Our apartment is in the basement.

The landlord opens the door, and after my eyes adjust to the dimness, I can see that this is the apartment in the pictures, only it looks smaller, more cellar-ish in person. I expected the apartment to be empty, waiting for us to move in, but it looks like someone still lives here.

As Gage and the man walk around, talking about the price of heat and electricity, I try to picture the two of us all moved in. On the orange counter is an old toaster oven and a monkey cookie jar. I wonder if the people who live here bought the cookie jar at the One Stop Party Shop. If so, maybe Briggs can get me one just like it. I'll fill it with peanut-butter cookies like the ones that Janna and I used to make. It was always my job to make crisscrosses across the top of the cookies with a fork. "Only two crisscrosses," Janna would say. When I'd ask why, she'd say, "Just because."

Instead of there being a cabinet below the sink, a brightly colored cloth hangs down to hide the stuff that's under there. I want to peek, but I don't want to be nosy.

Instead, I go look at the two bedrooms, trying to guess which one will be mine. I can tell from the furniture and decorations that an adult sleeps in one of the rooms and a boy and his baby sister in the other. The rooms look to be about the same size, but for whatever reason, I picture myself in the kids' bedroom. I imagine my bed pressed against one wall, which would leave room for a desk along the wall by the door. Maybe we could find a cheap desk on craigslist or somewhere. It doesn't have to be fancy — just someplace quiet for me to do homework.

Now I can't help myself: I decide to be nosy after all and look inside the closet. There isn't a bar inside the small closet for hanging clothes — just hooks against the back and the sides. But there is a book-shelf in the closet, where clothes have been folded and stuffed in. I bet Gage could put up a bar, though, if I asked him. Janna would want me to hang my uniforms on actual hangers, not on hooks. Besides, if I can hang some of my clothes on a bar, then I can use the bookshelf to set up my Paper Things. I'll have room for all three stories, and the top can be a rooftop terrace instead of a backyard. I'll be able to play Paper Things anytime I want, and no one will have to step around them. If I have Sasha over and don't want her to see them, I can just shut my closet door.

"Yeah, I think this will work," I hear Gage say, and I bounce up and down in my new room. I can't believe that we will have a place—*our very own place*—to come home to every night.

"Do you have the voucher?" the landlord asks. I stand next to Gage so I can hear all the details.

"Voucher?"

"From the Housing Authority."

I can tell that my brother is confused. He's pausing so the man will say more and he won't look ignorant.

"The rent on this apartment is subsidized. In order to live here, you have to have proof from the Housing Authority that your income falls below a certain level."

"Can't I just tell you what I make?" says Gage. "Or get my boss to write something? Trust me, it's low. Really low." He laughs, and so does the man.

"Yeah, I get you," says the landlord. "But the city has to make sure. I can't just rent this one out from under the people who have completed the paperwork and are still waiting for housing."

Gage's face shutters, like it used to do when Janna started in on him about something or other. I can tell that he's done listening, that he's given up hope.

"Where do we go to get the voucher?" I ask.

"The Housing Authority. But don't get your hopes up," he says to me. "It will take days, maybe even weeks, for you to qualify. Folks have been looking at this apartment since seven this morning; it'll be gone by tomorrow."

So now we're back on the streets, and once again I'm running in my flapping shoe, trying to keep up with my brother.

"Let's go to the Housing Authority right now!" I shout.

"It's closed, Ari!" he yells back to me like I don't know anything. "It's closed, and even if it were open, I don't know what I have to take there to prove that I make crap."

"Can't you just give them your boss's phone number? He'll tell them what you make."

"I just got the job; it's probably not even considered steady work yet. And what will I write when they ask for our current address?"

My mind starts working on possible answers — Janna's address or maybe Chloe's or Briggs's? Surely the Housing Authority people wouldn't follow up to verify that we lived there, right? But I don't make any suggestions. No idea will be the right one. No words will make Gage feel better. Not right now.

Eventually Gage's pace slows, and I catch up and walk by his side. I can tell that he's thinking. I want him to think out loud, but that isn't his style. Finally he turns to me and says in a voice much kinder than the one he's been using since we left the apartment, "You must have been scared when I didn't pick you up at Head Start."

I shrug like it was no big deal, but tears sting

my eyes. Now I'm the tired one. Tired of uncertainty. Tired of the unfamiliar. Tired of trying to figure things out. For a few moments I want to be five years old again. I want someone to plunk me in front of a Disney movie and ask, "Would you like apple juice or grape?"

"I'm so sorry, Ari," he says, and puts his arm around me. "So sorry. God, what if you hadn't found me? I messed up big time." He stops and turns me toward him. "Forgive me?"

"Maybe," I say, and he squeezes me against his side. "I need to call Carol," I add.

"I've been going back and forth in my head all day, but now I'm sure of it: we *have* to get a phone," he says.

What I want to say is *Talk to Janna. Tell her that we don't really have an apartment. Maybe she'll reactivate your phone.* But I don't. Instead I say, "Phones are *très* expensive."

"Not all of them," says Gage. "There are pay-as-you-go phones. Besides, a phone is not a luxury; it's a necessity. You need to be able to reach me. My boss needs to be able to reach me."

And Chloe, I think but don't say out loud. Something tells me Chloe's patience would run out altogether if she couldn't reach Gage when she wanted to. I start to ask Gage where he'll get the money, but I already know. The money will have to come from the first and last months' rent savings. Just an hour ago, it felt like we were so close to getting an apartment; now it feels like a lifetime away.

We ride the bus all the way out to Walmart, where it takes Gage forever to choose a phone. The pretty salesclerk tries to sell him a more expensive model — a phone with a data plan or a phone with flashy features. Gage keeps repeating the same thing: "I want the cheapest phone you have, and I want to keep my old number." The salesclerk doesn't think that keeping his number will be possible, but it's obvious that she likes Gage, and in the end — and after a ridiculously long call to our new telephone company — she finds a way.

Still, I can tell when we go to checkout and Gage pulls fifty dollars from his wallet that he feels anything but glad. I've often heard the expression *two steps forward, one step back.* Now I know what it means. That's what it's like trying to live on our own. Or maybe two steps forward and ten steps back.

I don't ask where we're sleeping tonight. I don't have to. When Gage is feeling beaten down, we stay away from friends. Being with friends who have jobs and apartments, he says, makes him feel like a loser.

The streets are getting darker. Headlights glare in my eyes. Tonight we're headed for the shelter.

· 21 ·
CHECKS

Technically, we're not allowed to stay at Lighthouse. First of all, you're supposed to be between twelve and twenty years old, so I don't qualify. Second of all, you're supposed to fill out paperwork when you check in, just like at the family shelter. But West doesn't make us register. He sneaks us into Lighthouse, which is not a lighthouse at all but an old-looking, three-story white-and-brown apartment house. The offices and kitchen are on the first floor. The second floor is the boys' floor, and the third floor is the girls'. Each floor holds up to eight kids, for a total of sixteen people per night. But West usually slips us into a little first-floor storage room, where we sleep on mats on the floor.

You would think that staying hidden downstairs would keep our stuff safer, but you'd be wrong. Kids are always raiding the downstairs rooms, looking for anything to take with them. So the first time when Gage and I left to use the bathrooms, stuff was taken. Now we know to leave the storage room one at a time. Fortunately, I can lock the door from the inside when Gage is gone.

We haven't had dinner, but we are on our way to Lighthouse anyway; West only works until eight and it must be getting close to that now.

About half a block away from Lighthouse, we stop in front of a parking garage so that Gage can call West. Only, for whatever reason, West doesn't answer. Gage tries again. Nothing.

"What's tonight?" he asks, but he doesn't wait for an answer. "West should be working."

Sleet starts to fall. I pull up my hood. My toes, especially the ones in the flappy shoe, are numb. I jump up and down to wake them back up. I'm hungry, but I don't say so. I wonder what the snack will be at Lighthouse tonight. I might ask West if he can grab me two shares before he leaves. That will make Gage mad, but I don't care; I was so busy making snowflakes that I hardly ate anything at Head Start.

"Arianna!" a man's voice calls from across the street.

I look around to see who might be calling me. For a moment, I'm convinced that this has something to do with West, that we're in trouble for trying to sneak into Lighthouse, though I know that's crazy.

And then I see who it is. Reggie, the airplane man, waves to me from across the street. Amelia is with him and she wags her tail when she sees me.

How lucky is this? "Hey, Reggie!" I call. "I was hoping to see you! I have something for you!"

Reggie crosses the street, and I try to introduce him to Gage, but Gage is concentrating on his frantic texting.

In a confetti toss of words, I tell Reggie about his plane, the cupola, Gage's new job, and Fran's bike plane, but he notices my teeth chattering and interrupts me to ask where we're headed. "I could walk with you while you tell me the whole story," he says.

"We're kind of hoping to stay there," I say, pointing to the shelter. But I can tell from Gage's eyes that he heard me and he wants me to shut up.

"Shelter full?" Reggie asks when Gage finally looks up from his phone.

Gage nods. I wonder what the real story is.

"Look," says Reggie, "I don't mean to be presumptuous, but I've got a place you can stay tonight. It's not the Taj Mahal, it's not even Motel Six, but it's warm."

"We appreciate the offer, sir," Gage starts to say, pulling his wool cap down lower. But Reggie interrupts him.

"You'd actually be doing me a favor. I'm hoping to stay at the men's shelter tonight—have a shower and maybe watch a little TV—but they don't allow dogs. If you could stay at my place and watch Amelia for me, I'd be grateful."

I look at Gage with pleading eyes, but he hesitates.

"It's pretty modest," Reggie says apologetically.

"There isn't even a proper bathroom, though I make do with a camping toilet. But it's dry and warm and no one will bother you." He goes on to explain that the place he rents is a heated storage unit down on Marginal Way. "I moved all my stuff in when I lost the house," he says. "It's a little crowded, but I've managed to set it up almost like an apartment."

"And you're not planning to stay there tonight?" Gage asks, sounding almost suspicious. I want to scold him for being so rude, but I remind myself that he doesn't know Reggie and Amelia like I do. Besides, Gage has never been one for trusting new people.

"I will if I have to," Reggie says. "I can't very well abandon this old girl," he says, reaching down to scratch Amelia behind the ears. "But I had been looking forward to that shower and to seeing some of my buddies at the shelter."

The wind picks up speed, and the sleet hits my face like a million tiny pinpricks. Finally I can't take it any longer. "Please say yes!" I shout, tugging on Gage's arm. "Please?"

Gage looks down at me, shrugs, and mutters, "OK, then. Thanks."

We follow Reggie across town to the storage units. First Reggie has to tap a code on a keypad clipped to a tall metal fence. After we go through the gate in the fence, he has to type the code into a box outside the door of a *très* big brick building, which looks kind of like a garage. Once we're inside, he leads us down a brightly lit hall of shed doors until we arrive at number 26. Then he taps in another code, and the door opens to reveal . . . boxes. All I can see is a wall of boxes. Boxes that seem to go all the way up to the tall ceiling.

I try to hide my disappointment, because I don't want to seem ungrateful, but I think Reggie was stretching the truth quite a bit to describe this place as apartment-like. To me it just looks like a storage shed. A very crowded storage shed.

But then Amelia leads us on a small path through the boxes—a path I hadn't even seen. Reggie motions for us to follow her, and so we do, and lo and behold, we come out into a long, skinny room set up just like an apartment!

Along the wall to the left is a camp cot. Next to the cot is a nightstand with a big flashlight on it, and beside that, a camouflage-print dog bed. Along the wall to the right is a long, narrow table. On the table is a plastic jug of water, a small coffeemaker, a cooking burner, and a toaster oven. Next to the table is a little refrigerator, the kind you see in back-to-school flyers advertising stuff for dorm rooms. On top of the refrigerator is a cooking pot, a cup and plate, and a pitcher full of cooking utensils. In the middle of the room sits a handsome coffee table. Right now, there's a model airplane being built on the coffee table—a plastic one, not a paper one. Reggie sure has a thing for planes.

A camping porta potty sits in the corner at the foot of the bed. "Like I said, it's pretty modest." Reggie sounds almost embarrassed.

"It's *wonderful!*" I say. Amelia wags her tail in agreement.

Reggie blushes and takes a mattress pad from a box and places it on the floor. He also retrieves a rolled-up sleeping bag and a few quilts, which he tosses onto the cot. "You guys hungry? I've got corned-beef hash or tuna noodles."

I nod, eager to see Reggie prepare a meal in this secret house. But Gage bristles.

"Hey, man," Gage says. "You don't have to feed us, too."

"It's my pleasure," says Reggie. "I'd rather eat with the two of you than some of the slobs at the shelter." He winks at me, and I smile in return.

While Reggie mixes up the Tuna Helper, he tells me where to dig for more dishes and cups. Mixed in among the boxes are a bicycle tire and pump, a pair of ski boots, and a plastic sled. The boxes themselves are filled with tools, pictures in frames, and candles. The candles make me think of electricity, and when I ask about it, Gage points out the outlet on the overhead light that powers this room.

"This place is great!" I say. "How much does it cost a month?"

"Ari," Gage snaps.

But Reggie doesn't seem to mind the question. "It's cheaper than renting an apartment," he says, "even Section Eight. But I don't recommend living in a storage unit if you can help it. It's hard to live without plumbing. Besides, it's technically against the law for me to sleep here. But it's against the law for me to sleep in the park or at the bus station, too, so what're you gonna do when the shelters are full?" he asks with a shrug.

"What's Section Eight?" I ask.

Gage speaks up. "It's like that apartment we saw tonight—units that are set aside for people who income-qualify."

I want to ask Reggie why he isn't living in the house where all this furniture came from, but I'm worried the question is too rude, and I don't want him to change his mind about letting us stay here.

Instead, I polish off my Tuna Helper and pull Fran's bicycle ad out of my backpack—along with her three dollars—and ask Reggie if he would make her an airplane, too. I tell him again about the wish I made on my plane and how it came true.

"She's paying me to make her a paper airplane?"

"Yup," I say. "But if you don't want to—"

"Oh, I don't mind doing it, and the money will

come in handy for dog food." He hands me back a dollar. "This one's for you, though," he says. "For being my business partner."

I shake my head. "Oh, no. She wanted you to have it."

"But I wouldn't have this job if not for you. You were the one who told your friend about the plane I gave you, and you were the one who came up with the idea of making a wishing plane."

I look at Gage, who nods that it's OK. "Thanks," I say, reluctantly taking the dollar. I can't help remembering that Reggie needed money for Amelia and wonder how he bought the tuna and how he pays the rent for his storage unit.

"Disability check," says Reggie, as if he's reading my mind. He begins to fold Fran's plane. "I get a check each month, but it's not enough to make it through thirty days."

"Were you in the service?" Gage asks.

Reggie nods. "Air force. A pilot."

"Our dad was in the army," Gage says.

"He was killed in Afghanistan," I say.

Reggie nods. "I'm sorry to hear that."

"Did you lose your house because of your disability?" Gage asks.

Now it's *my* turn to shoot *him* a look for being too nosy.

But again Reggie doesn't seem to mind the question. He hands me Fran's plane and says, "Yeah. You might say my disability led to the loss of a lot of things." Reggie is quiet, but then he looks up and smiles. "But I'm luckier than a lot of folks, and you can be sure I'm grateful for all that I've got—like new friends." He raises his cup of water to us.

"To new friends," Gage and I say together.

· 22 ·
SNOWFLAKES

After dinner, Reggie takes Amelia for a short walk and then says he'll be leaving for the shelter now but that he'll be back in the morning to pick up his girl.

He shows us how to keep the door locked from the inside, and then gives Gage the security codes to put in his phone, cautioning us not to leave without them.

After Reggie leaves, I call dibs on the mattress pad so I can cuddle with Amelia all night. There's no better feeling than looking into a dog's eyes. It's like they fetch all the love you can possibly throw out and then they give it back to you. That, and they seem to know all your secrets.

"Can we get a dog?" I ask. "When we get an apartment? It doesn't have to be a big dog like Amelia; it can be small like Leroy."

"No way," says Gage. "You heard Reggie. Dog food is expensive . . . and dogs need licenses and shots and a bunch of other stuff, too."

"But I'm collecting change—"

"Do you have homework tonight?" Gage interrupts. I can tell that he's tired and not in any mood to argue.

I do, but I lie. I'm tired, too. Too tired to work on my report, too tired to do my math, too tired even to play Paper Things. Besides, I've started rubbing Amelia's belly, and now she won't let me stop.

Gage turns out the light, and as I lie back on the mattress pad, I remember that I don't have a clean shirt in my backpack. My already-dirty shirt probably smells even worse after all the running around we did today. I guess that's another downside of living in a storage unit—no washing machine.

"No clean shirt tomorrow," I whisper to Amelia in the dark. It's just one more secret to her.

"You can wear the white one Briggs loaned me,"

Gage says, apparently still awake. "The one I wore to my interview."

"It'll be huge!" I say.

"It won't be *that* big. Wear it under your Tigers vest. It will look cute," he says. "I promise."

What choice do I really have? I can't very well wear a smelly shirt to school again, not after all the nasty comments Sasha and Linnie made last time. Though I'm sure I'll get an earful about how silly I look wearing a man's shirt.

Sometimes there's just no winning, I think at Amelia, rubbing her belly till my eyes drift shut.

Gage's new phone rings at some ridiculously early hour—or at least I think it's a ridiculously early hour; who can tell when you're sleeping in a box without windows?

"Who?" growls Gage into the phone.

I think it's a wrong number, but then he hands the phone to me.

"Hello?"

It's Daniel. "Have you looked outside?"

"No, I—"

"It's snowing!"

In Maine, snow in April, especially at the beginning of the month, is no big deal. I remember one time we got snow in June. So it takes me a moment or two to realize what he's suggesting.

"Will we be ready?" I ask. "I made some snowflakes yesterday at Head Start, but probably only fifty or so."

"That's perfect! I made a bunch last night, too. I think we must have known snow was coming!"

"Yeah, I guess so," I say, though really, I was just happy to have a new activity to share with the Starters.

"Can you meet me at the school in half an hour?" Daniel says. "That should give us plenty of time to set things up."

"What time is it, anyway?" I ask, glancing at Gage, who is moaning under his pillow.

"Six. Let's hope the building opens this early, or we're sunk."

Gage isn't too keen on letting me leave the warehouse without him—though it's far too early for him to show up at work. He offers to walk me to the bus stop, but I remind him that we can't leave Amelia alone in the storage unit (if she barked or howled, she'd be discovered and taken away from Reggie—and he'd probably lose the storage unit, too), and Reggie might be really upset if he got back and not only were we gone but so was his dog. "Besides," I add, "I'm eleven. That's old enough to walk to the bus stop by myself."

I can tell that Gage wants to argue some more, but eventually he gives me Briggs's big white shirt to wear and lets me go.

Daniel is standing outside Eastland when I arrive. My feet are soaked, but I'm too nervous to mind. "Did you bring tape?" I ask him.

"Of course," he says. Thankfully, he doesn't ask me why I didn't bring any.

Daniel strides up to the front door and gives it a confident tug. But nothing happens. He frowns and tries again.

"Locked!" he says, like he can't believe the door wouldn't be open at six thirty in the morning.

"What now?" I ask, stamping my feet to try to warm them.

Daniel looks around and then smiles. "Tracks!" he says, pointing to large footprints in the snow—footprints that definitely don't belong to either of us. We follow them with our eyes from the front door back up the walkway and to the parking lot, where the janitor's car is parked. A thin layer of snow dusts the windshield, though the hood is clear—probably because it's still warm.

"Come on," Daniel says, walking around the building. "She's gotta be in here somewhere!"

Sure enough, we see someone vacuuming in one of the third-grade rooms. We rap on the window and the vacuuming stops.

As the figure approaches, I see that it's not Mrs. Hurley, the janitor, but Yan, her helper. I wonder if he walked to the school or if he and Mrs. Hurley carpooled. Anyway, he frowns when he sees us and motions for us to go back around the corner to the nearest door.

He opens the door just a crack, his frown

deepening. It's clear that he doesn't really want to let us in. My stomach ties a knot or two.

"Eastland tradition," says Daniel, as if he's twenty and not eleven. "We've got to hang up snowflakes today."

Yan has only worked for Mrs. Hurley for a few months, so I'm not sure what he makes of this talk of *tradition* and *snowflakes,* but he slowly steps aside to let us pass.

"Be good!" he calls as we tear down the hall toward the front office.

Being in the school when no one else is here is both really cool and very eerie. Now more than ever I feel like a ghost—though a ghost with a friend this time. I think of the things we could get away with right now: sneaking into the teachers' lounge, rearranging desks in classrooms, hanging safety posters upside down. If I wasn't trying so hard to get into Carter, I might suggest some of these things to Daniel.

I wonder if this is what it's like for kids like Linnie, who don't have to worry about being good all the time, because they don't care about getting into Carter. Is life a lot more relaxing and fun when you don't have to try so hard?

Daniel quickly surveys the window outside the front office. "Help me pull this bench over and we can begin up high."

Before you know it, the front hall of our school has been blitzed with snowflakes. Just like old times, snowflakes appear to float from the ceiling to the floor in the main hall. It looks amazing, and I can't wait for everyone to see it, especially Sasha.

"We've still got an hour before school starts," Daniel says. "Want to make more?"

"Snowflakes?" I ask stupidly. "Where would we put them?" The walls and windows of the main hall are practically filled with flakes already.

"Anywhere!" Daniel says.

His enthusiasm is catching. "We could put some in Mr. O.'s room," I suggest. "He always liked the snowflake tradition. And maybe in the cafeteria, too."

We head down to the art room for scissors and raid the recycling bins for paper. "Don't be too particular about these," Daniel says as we start folding and cutting at the large art room table. "It's the overall effect we want." So we mass-produce the easiest snowflakes we can. They're not very fancy, but we've learned to cut more than one at a time, and soon they're piling up.

We finish decorating Mr. O.'s room in record time and move on to the cafeteria. We can hear movement now in the hallways — teachers and students arriving — and we start taping even faster than before. At one point we're almost caught, when Ms. Finch walks by the doors, but we duck behind the tables and she doesn't see us.

Ten minutes before the bell is supposed to ring, we head to the hall where our lockers are located, acting like we've just arrived. But my stomach is jumping like it's Christmas morning.

The school looks amazing. I can't believe that we were able to hang so many dazzling snowflakes, that in less than two hours we created this wintry magic. Sasha approaches me with Keisha at her side. I wonder where Linnie is. Has Sasha ditched her, too, and moved on to Keisha?

I hold my breath, waiting to hear what Sasha has to say. Will she know that the snowflakes were my doing? It's weird to keep such a big secret from my best friend—or maybe my former best friend.

To my surprise, Keisha grabs my arm. "Hey, Ari," she says. "That shirt looks really cool. Doesn't it, Sasha? Where'd you get it?"

At first I worry that she's making fun of me. Briggs's shirt was just as big as I'd feared it would be, though I'd worn it under my vest as Gage had suggested and rolled up the sleeves. Maybe the look *was* pretty cool. "I borrowed it from a friend," I say mysteriously.

"Cool," Keisha says again. Sasha just gives me a wide-eyed look.

I smile and turn to head into math. I decide to keep my secrets just a little bit longer.

· 23 ·
TOWELS

I'm in my seat, trying madly to complete last night's math homework before the bell rings, while still listening to the reactions to the snowflakes. I can't help it.

Most of the kids are guessing that adults did it—either the PTO or the basketball boosters or something.

Some kids are a little grouchy about it. "It was fun when *we* got to do the snowflakes," they complain.

Their reactions make me realize that we probably should have involved more kids from the beginning.

Class is just about to begin when Mr. Chandler's voice comes over the loudspeaker. "Would the young man and the young lady who decided to enter the school unlawfully this morning and, further, deface school property come to the office immediately."

Unlawfully? Deface?

I glance at Daniel. Neither of us moves.

A few minutes later, Mr. Chandler's voice comes over the loudspeaker again. "Would Daniel Huber and Arianna Hazard please come to the office?"

My wobbly knees are not to be trusted, but I stand up. Out of the corner of my eye, I see Daniel doing the same. The kids around us are shocked. "Ari?" I hear Sasha gasp, and I don't dare look at her. Daniel and I grab our backpacks and head for the door.

"How does he know it's us?" I ask as soon as we're in the hall. "I didn't think Yan even knew who we were."

"There's probably a security camera," says Daniel. "I can't believe I didn't think of it."

"What do you think is going to happen?" My stomach is back to doing flip-flops, and that's when I remember that I didn't have any breakfast this morning. I didn't pack a lunch, either. Not that I can imagine eating a thing.

"I don't know," says Daniel. "But think about what you're going to say to Mr. Chandler. Why are Eastland traditions important?"

I try to think of this like an essay for Carter. If I had to explain why I wanted to reinstate the traditions at Eastland Elementary, what would I say? Maybe something about how traditions give us a sense of belonging, that doing the same activities each year, the very same activities that our older siblings or even our parents did, makes us feel like we're all one big family. And events like the fifth-grade campout give us something to look forward to as we grow older.

But rather than feeling prepared, I feel a little light-headed. My stomach continues cramping. I don't know how I'm ever going to survive this meeting.

Mr. Chandler stands at the end of the hall, watching us approach. He's wearing that look that parents and teachers have when they're disappointed in you, and I can't help feeling that it's directed more at me than at Daniel. While Daniel has "visited" the principal's office regularly since kindergarten, including more than a few times this year with Mr. Chandler (as Mademoiselle likes to say, Daniel is always thinking outside the box), I've never actually been sent to the office. Up until now, I've been known to Mr. Chandler as "Janna's girl." Janna is one of those people who always volunteers— mostly, I think, because she likes to be the boss. I wonder if Mr. Chandler has noticed that she's stopped volunteering lately.

"Does Janna know what you were up to this morning?" he asks once we reach him.

"No, sir," I say, my voice quavering. How am I ever going to get through my speech?

He takes a breath, leans back on his heels, and digs his hands deeper into his pockets. "Do you two know the hours that Mrs. Hurley and Yan will need to spend to get glitter off these recently polished floors?" At this, he lifts his shoe to reveal the glitter that has stuck to it.

I shoot Daniel a guilty look. The only snowflakes with glitter had been mine.

Mr. Chandler continues without waiting for an answer. "It was one thing to enter the building before school started and to post paper and tape on the walls of school property. But to create hours and hours of extra work for two people who already work quite hard—well, that's truly unfair."

Daniel screws his face up, and I can't tell if he's thinking, *A few sparkles never hurt anyone,* or *It was pretty stupid, Ari, to make snowflakes with glitter,* or something else entirely.

"Follow me," says Mr. Chandler, and he leads us toward the custodian's closet.

"Speak up," Daniel whispers to me.

I widen my eyes and shrug my shoulders. What could I possibly say? Mr. Chandler is right about the glitter; it was inconsiderate.

He unlocks the closet and turns to us. "First I want you to take the snowflakes down, and then I want you to use these mops to get the glitter off the floor."

"Say something, Ari," Daniel whispers when Mr. Chandler heads down the hall ahead of us. "He's making an example of us." I can tell that Daniel's pretty bummed right now.

My stomach lurches. "Mr. Chandler," I say. It comes out as a squeak, so I try again. "Mr. Chandler—"

He turns and looks at me.

"We didn't mean to cause extra work. The glitter is my fault. I didn't realize—"

I stop. My stomach is lurching. Before I even know what's happening, a huge wave of tuna-noodle casserole rises from my belly, explodes past my tonsils, and sprays down the hall at a record distance.

I crouch over, holding my stomach and crying, but not before I see the splat on Mr. Chandler's pant leg and the look of horror on his face. I know Daniel well enough to know that there's probably a look of sheer delight on his.

I don't dare move, but I can hear Mr. Chandler directing his secretary to make three phone calls: one to Mrs. Hurley, one to the school nurse, and the other—before I can think how to stop him—to Janna.

· 24 ·
PHOTOGRAPHS

The first time I wake up, I've forgotten that we ever left Janna's. My old flannel nightgown, the one I love even though there's a hole in the elbow, is wrapped around me. I pull the down comforter up to my chin and glance around the room, listening for familiar voices, wondering whether it's a school day, whether Janna is going to pop her head into the room and tell me to get my sweet butt out of bed.

And then I remember.

I remember throwing up on Mr. Chandler's leg, burning up in the nurse's office while waiting for Janna to come. I remember Janna placing an arm around me and leading me to the car. I remember her suggesting I sit in the front seat and handing me plastic shopping bag in case I needed to throw up again. I wanted her to tease me, to say something funny to help make up for the humiliation of what had just happened, like Gage would have. I wanted her to say, "God, I've missed you." But she didn't.

The second time I wake up, I don't have to remind myself of what happened; my stomach is doing a repeat performance. I lean over and puke into the trash can. I don't want to think of Janna, of where she might be or what she'll say when she comes into the room and smells the vomit. Instead, I think of Gage. What time of day is it? Did he go to Head Start to pick me up? Has anyone told him where I am? But these worrisome thoughts mix with my feverish dreams and I fall back to sleep again.

I can tell now that it's morning. Janna is standing over me with a spoonful of canned pineapple juice. It's what she always gave us for an upset stomach: canned fruit juice *only*, until we declared we were starving. Then she knew it was OK for us to put something in our stomachs. I lean up on my elbows to get the juice into my mouth. I feel like a baby bird when she feeds me this way. "Gage?" I say as soon as I've swallowed.

I can tell by her expression that his name shouldn't have been the first thing out of my mouth. "Thanks" would have gone over a whole lot better.

"He knows you're here. I left a message on his phone before picking you up."

"Thank you. For coming to pick me up, I mean," I say, in case she thinks I'm just talking about Gage again.

Janna nods. "You've got the flu," she says. "The nurse said it was going around."

I groan weakly and let my head fall back onto the pillow. The pillow with its clean white pillowcase, one that still smells mountain fresh even though I've no doubt drooled all over it.

"I can't stay home today," she says. "I've got to get to work. Do you think you can fend for yourself?"

Now I'm the one who nods. I've never stayed alone when I was sick before. Janna, a medical transcriptionist, always worked from home — typing up reports from recordings that doctors sent her. "I'm eleven," I remind us both.

"I'll leave this here," she says, placing the can of pineapple juice next to me. "See if you can't make it to the toilet if you need to throw up again."

"May I watch TV?" I ask. I expect her to say no—she's pretty strict about staying in bed on sick days, and I'm not even sure I *want* to watch TV— but asking feels just like old times, when Janna was my guardian and I would ask her permission to turn on the television or play a game on her computer.

"What would Gage say?" she asks, and leaves the room.

I can't decide if that was a serious question—if she wants me to act like I would if Gage were in charge, since I'm living with him now—or if it's her way of saying, "You're not mine anymore, so what do I care?"

I listen to the sounds of her leaving: the emptying of the coffeepot, the rinsing of her breakfast dishes before she stacks them in the dishwasher, the click of the dishwasher door. She pounds her feet into her boots, and then the kitchen door shuts: once loosely, then tightly. I think about getting up and making sure that the door is locked, which is silly. Janna always locks the door.

I feel drained, empty like the coffeepot. I look around my old room, which hasn't changed much in the months we've been gone. The white furniture is the same; my books are still on the shelves. The only difference is that the framed pictures are gone. There is no picture of me and Sasha on my eighth birthday, no picture of seven-year-old Gage holding me when I was born, no picture of me and Janna and Gage on the day she took us to court to get official guardianship.

I remember telling Sasha once that Janna had adopted us and Gage correcting me angrily. "Not adopted," he'd said, his face like storm clouds. "Adopting is when someone becomes a parent. Janna is just our guardian." I never understood why this upset him so much; Janna did all the things a parent was supposed to do and signed all the same forms, and who could blame her for not wanting to become our parent? After all, our track record with parents wasn't very good.

I get up to use the bathroom, and then I walk around Janna's house, running my finger along familiar (and always dust-free) surfaces: the windowsills, the glass coffee table, the granite countertop. Despite the fact that I should only be sipping on pineapple juice, I look in the baking cupboard to see if there are any chocolate chips. Whenever Gage and I were alone, we'd snatch some, always careful to take only a few so Janna wouldn't be able to tell. Janna does have a bag of Nestlé Semi-Sweet Morsels, but it isn't open. I place it back in the cabinet in its exact place.

Gage's room is upstairs with Janna's—both of their rooms are larger than mine. I start to look into Gage's room but then stop myself. Seeing his things might make me feel sad. And what if Janna has changed his room, moved his things? That would make me even sadder.

I peek into Janna's room, where we've never been allowed. Janna called her room the "sanctuary"—a place where she could be alone and do the things she used to do BK (before kids), like painting her toenails and working on her scrapbooks. I see that there, on the end of her bed, is a neat pile of magazines and catalogs. She used to save them for me, and I wonder if she still does. I sit on the edge of the bed (careful not to make wrinkles) and look through a Mini Boden. There is a page that says, "Bonnie for Babies," and it has the cutest little kids I've ever seen. There is an African-American toddler boy with a red snowflake sweater and a smile that makes my weak body feel stronger. There's a white toddler girl in a colorful dress with two sleepy owls on the front who looks as if she's about to take her very first step. I decide to cut the kids out and add them to the day care where Miles and Natalie go. And then, just like old times, I'm going to spread my Paper Things all over my old room. I'm going to play for hours.

I bravely tear the pages out of the catalog, so neatly that Janna might not even notice. Before leaving Janna's room, I wander from corner to corner, peeking at the pictures of her parents and her sisters on the wall, and the items — perfume, lotion, earring tree, cotton balls — placed ever so carefully on her bureau and vanity. I wander over to the table against the wall, where she keeps her scrapbooks and her carefully organized scrapbooking tools.

There are lots of brightly colored papers, and scissors that will cut the paper edges with zigzags or curly scallops. There are also stickers, lots and lots of stickers, of things like barbecue grills, tall glasses of lemonade, and watermelon; clearly Janna is working on summer pages in her scrapbook. I used to wish I could use some of those stickers for my Paper Things, but Janna's scrapbook stuff was always off-limits. In fact, I've never even looked through any of the books. She used to say, "Someday, when you're older, I'll show you them," but she never did.

Now I'm home alone for the first time, and I can't help wondering what it was that she didn't want to share. I know it's wrong, but I can't stop thinking that this might be the only chance I'll ever have to see her scrapbooks—and she *did* intend for me to see them, someday.

I sit down in her chair, pull it up to the table, and open the nearest one.

The book begins with old baby pictures, the corners of the pictures rounded like the ones Mama had of her and Dad back in high school. It takes me a second to recognize Janna's mother, who always asked us to call her Nana. She's much younger in the pictures and looks like Janna does now. The baby must be Janna. Then there are pictures of Janna as a toddler taking her first steps, Janna as a preschooler asleep with a book on her chest, Janna at her six-year-old birthday party, riding a pony.

I feel a pang as I flip through the scrapbook; Gage and I don't have baby albums of any kind. Mama always said that our dad wasn't home long enough to take any pictures of us when we were babies and she was just too plain tired to take any herself. But someone at some point took a few pictures, because I remember seeing ones of baby Gage running around the house without clothes, me in a high chair with baby food smeared all over my face, and toddler me crying because Gage had left the room. I wonder whatever happened to those pictures.

I flip through more of the scrapbook. There are pages with tickets, notes from friends, some report cards (all A's and some A+'s), and a picture of Janna in a straw hat with a huge polka-dotted bow, next to the one of my mother with her pipe-cleaner hat.

Eventually I come to Janna's high-school years.

There's a page for field hockey, and I recognize my mother in a few of the pictures. Another page is devoted to prom. Janna's pressed her corsage into the book. Even all dried and brown tinged, it's still pretty. I take a closer look at a picture of Janna in her prom dress to see what the corsage looked like when the flowers were fresh. It was a burst of pink daisies tied up with a hot-pink bow. The bow matches the ribbon around Janna's lacy pink-and-white dress. Janna looks so young, and she's wearing an expression that I've rarely seen on her before: a full smile, which lights up her whole face.

I look over at her boyfriend, wondering who this guy was who made Janna so happy.

At first I think it's Gage. *What the—?*

Slowly, though, I realize that it's not my brother's face staring back at me but my father's.

Holy moly, Janna's prom date was my dad!

I stare for a good long while, as if expecting the image to change. Eventually, though, I turn the page.

Next come pictures of Janna and my mom. I half expect them to look tense in these pictures—surely

Mama couldn't have been happy that her best friend was going to prom with her future husband!—but in every picture they are laughing, usually with their arms around each other. I trace my fingers over Mama's smiling face. She didn't look that different when I knew her—thinner and sadder, sure, but not much older. She was only thirty-two when she died.

I continue flipping through the pages. There are more pictures of Janna and my dad. Lots more. Janna and my dad at other dances, hugging at a basketball game, smiling at Nana's Thanksgiving table, showing off their Christmas presents.

My confusion grows as each memory passes by. My parents were married right after high school. When did Janna and my dad stop being a couple? When did my mom and dad start? And why didn't anyone ever mention that Janna used to date my dad?

I can't stop examining every detail on these pages, and I quickly notice something. As I get closer and closer to graduation, all of the pictures that include my mom or dad have tear marks through them, though they've been carefully taped back together. Whatever happened with my mom and dad and Janna had clearly upset Janna at the time.

I close the scrapbook and decide not to look through the others. I already know way more than I wanted to know—though at the same time, I feel like I don't know anything at all.

25

PLAYING CARDS

"You're eleven," says Janna. She's standing in the doorway to my room. I freeze, my paper mom in one hand and Natalie in the other. "Don't you think it's about time you stopped playing with paper dolls?"

I feel caught. Caught-with-my-hands-in-the-chocolate-chips-bag caught. I shrug.

Janna sits down on the edge of my bed, like there's nothing she'd rather be doing than watching me play Paper Things—though I know that's not the case.

But I can't play Paper Things with her there. My paper world is my private world; it doesn't work if there are people watching me.

"How was work?" I ask, placing my people down on the plush couch in my home.

"Busy," she says.

"What do you do?"

She opens her arms, looks down at her uniform, and then up at me.

I should have noticed. "You're a nurse?" I ask.

"Really, Ari. It's as if you and Gage think I didn't exist before I took you in. Of course I'm a nurse."

"Do you work at the hospital?"

"I worked in the ER before I became a medical transcriptionist. Now I work in a nursing home."

"At Parkers?" I ask. That's where Gage used to work sometimes, the place where Mr. Lynnfield cheats at cards.

"No, not Parkers. How are you feeling?"

"Somewhat better," I say. I have a little quilt wrapped around my legs, and my pillow is here on the floor with me. "When the room starts to spin, I just lie down for a while."

"Back in bed," she says, which is what I was afraid she'd say. I pull myself up and start to crawl under the covers.

"Oh, no, pick these up first," she says, sweeping her arm around the whole room. "You won't like it if I come in during the night and end up stomping all over them."

I wake when Janna strides in with a mug of chicken soup and a handful of crackers.

"What's it like, living in a studio?" she asks as I blow on the soup to cool it.

The question catches me off guard, and I'm glad to have the excuse of the soup to buy me more time. I hate lying, but Gage fooled Janna into believing we have an apartment, and I don't want to get him in trouble. "It's cozy. We can't spread our things out, though, or the place turns into a real mess," I say, staying as close to the truth as possible.

Janna is giving me her I-thought-so look.

And then, for who knows what reason, I blurt out, "Were you and Mama friends for a long time?"

"Your mother was my best friend in high school," she says. "I've told you that."

I want to ask a gazillion more important

questions, questions like: How come you never told me that my dad was your boyfriend? And when did he become Mama's boyfriend? And is this why you and Mama weren't friends when Gage and I were growing up? And how did it feel when Mama called you and told you she was dying and that she wanted to make up—oh, and would you mind raising her two children, since her own folks were dead and our dad's parents had never even met us? (Gage told me once that they'd disapproved of our dad marrying Mama. I wonder now if it was because they'd been hoping he'd marry Janna instead.)

But I can't ask Janna any of these questions because I wasn't supposed to be in her room, snooping in her scrapbook. Not that she'd likely have answered my questions anyway.

I spend the whole weekend with Janna. She doesn't have to work, so we watch HGTV together. Her favorite show is about a bickering couple. The woman is a decorator and she remodels people's homes. While she's fixing the home up, the man is busy trying to persuade the home owners to sell their house and move somewhere else. My favorite show is House Hunters, which is about people like me and Gage looking for the perfect home. I always try to guess which house the people will choose, and most of the time I'm right. Janna tells me I have an eye for real estate, which makes me happy.

On Sunday, I'm feeling mostly better—except for a cough and a nose that won't stop running. I go to bed early and lie awake awhile, wondering if Gage and Janna have talked, wondering how long I'm going to stay at Janna's. I've just drifted off to sleep when I'm awakened by Gage's voice. At first I'm not sure if I'm awake or dreaming.

"Welcome to the real world," I hear Janna say. "What did you *think* was going to happen?"

"I didn't think that . . ." Gage stops and sighs.

It's not a dream. I sit up high on my pillow, trying to listen. I can only hear what they're saying when they raise their voices.

"Just for a little while." That's Gage.

What would be just for a little while? Are we moving back? I get out of bed and stumble closer to the door.

"It can't always be about you, Gage. What *you* need."

"It's not about me! This is about Ari!"

Silence.

Janna mumbles something, and then I hear her say, "You know the terms: if she stays, you can't come back in a week or a month and tell me she's moving in with you again. If she stays, she stays for good. I can't go through this again."

If she *stays? Gage wants me to stay? Just me? With no chance of being a family again?* I suddenly have difficulty breathing. I crack open my door, wanting to hear more while I quickly pack up my things.

"We're supposed to stay together," Gage is saying, but he sounds defeated.

"Your mother never meant for Ari to suffer the way she has these past weeks. You and I both know that."

I've heard about enough. I grab my backpack and walk into the living room. Janna is sitting in the chair by the gas fireplace. Gage is standing, zipping up his coat.

I walk over to Gage and take his hand.

"You're OK," he says, sounding relieved. I wonder what Janna must have told him to make him look so worried. I squeeze his hand.

"I'm ready to go," I say.

After what feels like an eternity, Gage gives a decisive nod. "I was only asking for a little more time to put everything in place," he says to Janna. "But as usual, things have to be on your terms."

We head over to the door to get my shoes. I reach down to put them on, and my finger pokes through the hole in the stitching. Gage grabs them out of my hand. "You can put them on outside," he says. "So you won't leave any tracks in here." But I know the real reason is that he doesn't want Janna to notice what sorry shape they're in.

And I realize that today, unlike the day we left, I really made a choice. I chose to go with my brother rather than stay with Janna. Suddenly I feel more sad than angry. No matter which way I turn, I have to say good-bye to someone I care about. To someone I love.

I run back and give Janna a hug.

"Ari—" Janna starts, but Gage pulls me out the door before she can finish.

26

RENTAL AGREEMENTS

"You're not going to school, Ari," Gage says later that morning when I walk out of Briggs's bathroom in my school uniform. (Thank goodness we have clean laundry at Briggs's. I wonder what Janna did with my shirt—Briggs's shirt—that I threw up on.)

"I feel better," I say, which is somewhat true; showering always makes me feel better. "Besides, if I don't go, I'm going to fall further behind."

"You're behind?" Gage asks, putting his chair-bed back together.

"Some," I say. I haven't wanted Gage to know how far behind. I don't want him to think that I haven't been working as hard as he has to keep on top of things.

"Then stay and get caught up," Gage says. "If you go to school and have a relapse, they'll call Janna again."

"Why can't you just tell them to call you?" I ask, though I think I know the answer.

"You know why, B'Neatie," he says, trying for a teasing tone, but I can tell he's not feeling especially playful right now. "So just stay here and rest up. And catch up, too."

"Stay," says Briggs, sitting on the arm of the love seat while attaching his One Stop Party Shop name tag to his shirt. "You can play your paper game."

"No, she can't," says Gage. "If she's well enough to be up, she's well enough to do schoolwork." He sounds just like Janna when he says this, though no way am I going to point that out.

"Then you can use my laptop," says Briggs. "To do research or type up any assignments. But no matter what you do, remember to keep things quiet. I don't want the landlord to know that you're here — especially when I'm not."

I sink down onto the love seat, slightly relieved. It will be great not to have to figure out who to sit with at lunchtime, or not to have to face everyone after the snowflake-and-projectile-vomit fiasco— especially Mr. Chandler. And it will be nice, too, if I can actually finish my report on Louisa May Alcott.

"Oh, I almost forgot," says Gage, reaching into his Jiffy Lube shirt pocket. "Janna gave me this." He pulls out a slip of paper that practically glows. He doesn't have to tell me or Briggs what it is. Anyone who's gone to Eastland knows that a half sheet of paper the color of a pumpkin means one thing: detention.

Tears sock my eyes. I can't believe that I actually got detention! "But we were trying to do a good thing," I say.

"Yeah, but you trespassed on school property. If I had known that's what you and that Daniel kid were up to—"

But Briggs cuts him off. "You're hardly the first Hazard to serve detention as an Eastland Tiger. Your brother was known to bend the rules from time to time himself. Or have you forgotten, dude?"

I look up at their smirking faces. They're clearly remembering some pranks Gage pulled back in the day, when Gage was goofier. Back when Mama was alive.

"Yeah, but it looks like I'll be the first Hazard not to go to Carter," I say.

Gage's smile disappears.

"You'll go to Carter," says Briggs, knocking me playfully on the back of the head. "'Cause you're a smart aleck. Now get over here and eat your Cheerios."

Gage has to leave first. He stands too long at the door, and I know that he feels nervous about leaving me alone. "I'll come back at lunchtime to check up on you," he says.

"There's not much here to eat," Briggs says. He opens the refrigerator door to reveal two beers, the remaining milk, and a container of sour-cream-and-onion dip.

"I'll pick something up," says Gage.

"And still get back to South Port City on time?" says Briggs. "It's your second week on the job.

There's no way you can get here and back on the bus in an hour."

"I'll be OK," I say to Gage. "You don't need to come back. I'll have more Cheerios for lunch."

Gage isn't convinced.

"You can call me to check in," I say. "Call me at lunchtime."

The alligator lights and the smiley-face rugs stare at me now that the guys are gone. I reach into my backpack, intending to pull out my biography of Louisa May Alcott, but my Paper Things folder catches my eye and I pull it out instead. The folder is so worn and dirty that it feels more like cotton than card stock. Someday I'd like to buy a binder with more pockets. Then I could divide up my families, furniture, and the day care.

I run my fingers over the familiar faces and objects in my Paper Things folder, saying hello to these images that have been such a big part of my life for so many years. I would really like to spread everything out on Briggs's floor (maybe after giving it a quick vacuum), but I promised Gage I'd work on my report today. With a sigh, I put the folder back and pull my copy of *Little Women* out of my backpack. I want to add more quotes from the book to support the section of my report where I talk about what a great writer Louisa May Alcott was.

I write my new pages on Briggs's computer and then start typing up the pages I wrote over lunch in Mr. O.'s room. It's pretty slow going, though, because I'm not the fastest typist in the world. Plus, I have to keep stopping to blow my nose.

Around lunchtime, I decide to give my fingers a rest, even though I'm not really hungry yet. I get up and look out the window. Pine Street below is busy, and it's fun to spy on people when they have no idea you're watching them. There are lots of people around Gage's age who go by, and some mothers— or maybe nannies—with young children. It's sunny out, and warmer than it's been. People are peeling off their scarves and unzipping their jackets as they walk. It's hard to believe that it was snowing just a few days ago. One little kid has rubber boots on and is pulling his mother's hand so he can jump in every single puddle.

Just when I'm about to turn back to the computer, I see a woman I know. At first I can't place her; she has on a fuzzy hat and her head is down, but her walk looks so familiar. And then, as she passes, it hits me: it's Fran! Fran from Head Start. I rush to my backpack, and then out the door.

She hears me on my third shout, turns around, and walks back up the hill toward me. "Ari! What a surprise," she says. "We've missed you at Head Start." Then she notices what I'm wearing. "You're dressed for school, but you're not in school."

"Gage wouldn't let me go today. I've had the flu and he wants to make sure I'm over it."

"Good idea," says Fran, shifting her messenger bag from one shoulder to the other. "But shouldn't you be wearing a coat?"

"I'm OK," I assure her. "It's nice out, and I only came outside to give you this." I hold Reggie's plane out to her.

"Oh, wow!" Fran takes the plane and examines it closely. "It's a beauty! He's one talented guy, your airplane man."

"It's a Hell Plane," I tell her. "He chose it for you

because it has two points, the way a bicycle has two wheels."

Fran smiles. "I almost hate to let it go," she says. "Where do you think I should fly it?"

"Are you walking to Head Start now?" I ask.

Fran nods. "Well, to the bus stop," she clarifies.

I try to picture a high place between here and the bus stop. "There's that church nearby—the big white one. Maybe you can get up into the bell tower."

I expect Fran to dismiss this idea, but instead she seems to be considering it.

"I can come with you, if you want," I offer. This definitely sounds like more fun than typing, and I'd love to see Reggie's Hell Plane fly.

She laughs, and I realize that I don't hear Fran laugh much. Now, Carol, she laughs all the time, but Fran, she keeps her feelings more to herself. "I don't think that's what your brother has in mind for you today. In fact, you'd better get back inside. It may be a nice day, but you can still catch a chill."

She thanks me again for the plane and has me promise to tell Reggie how grateful she is to him. We say our good-byes, and I head back into the apartment building. As I trudge my still-wobbly legs up the stairs, it occurs to me that Fran must live in the same neighborhood as Briggs. It probably takes her an hour to get to Head Start, between the walk to the center of Port City and the bus ride to the East End. Now I know why she's so desperate to get a bike; if she had a bike, she could ride directly down Commercial Street and be in the East End in a third of the time—maybe even less.

I arrive at the door of Briggs's apartment and turn the doorknob. It doesn't turn.

I use both hands to twist the knob as hard as I can, but of course it still doesn't turn. It's locked.

I push on the door, hoping it didn't really shut all the way, that the force of my push will make the door pop open. It doesn't.

I try the doorknob again.

The door is locked. I don't have a key. And Gage and Briggs aren't going to be back for hours. Oh, and I can't go to the landlord—even if I knew which unit was his—because Gage and I aren't supposed to be staying here anymore.

Despite the warmer weather outdoors, it's cold in this hall. I don't know anyone in the building. I don't have a coat. I haven't eaten any lunch.

Just then, the phone rings inside the apartment. It's probably Gage, calling to see if I'm OK.

Holy moly, what have I gotten myself into?

I hear footsteps coming down the hall. What if it's the landlord? I dash back down the stairs and out the door so I won't be seen near Briggs's apartment.

A man leaves, but I have no idea if it was the landlord or not.

Not knowing what else to do, I crouch against the wall of the building across the street. People glance at me as they pass by, and I can tell that they're wondering if they should stop, wondering if they should do something for me. But no one does.

An hour passes, maybe more. The day starts to get cooler, and a fog rolls in. I can't afford to get sick again.

Reluctantly, I go back inside, where I lean against Briggs's door. And wait.

· · ·

I'm folded up, my head on my knees. It seems like hours have passed, though I'm not sure how many, when suddenly I hear Gage's voice.

"What are you doing out here, Ari?" He is as angry as I feared.

That's when I start to cry. Up until this moment, I was just worried, worried and cold. But now I am sobbing. "I saw Fran and ran out to give her the airplane."

"Why didn't you take a key?"

"I didn't think of it. I'm sorry."

"You didn't think at all, Ari!" he shouts. He looks around quickly, and I can tell he's remembering the warning about the landlord. He lowers his voice, but it still hits me like fists. "I kept calling and you didn't answer. I had to leave work early. It's only my second week, and I had to tell them that I had a family emergency!"

I don't think I've ever seen Gage this mad, this disappointed in me.

"I'm sorry, I'm sorry," I repeat between sobs. "I thought of asking someone on the street if I could use their phone, but I was afraid you'd come home if you knew that I was locked out. I didn't want you to get in trouble."

"Well, you should have thought of that before you ran out!"

"I know!" I sob. "I know!"

Gage sighs an enormous sigh and then slides down to sit next to me.

"It's not your fault. It's mine," he says, resting his head on the door. And then to my surprise, a tear runs down his cheek, too. "I'm the one who lied to Janna and said we had an apartment. I'm the one who drags you all over the city, carrying all your belongings in your backpack. I'm the one who gets mad at you when you're sick, who can't give you more than Cheerios for breakfast and for lunch."

"I don't care about any of that," I say, and I mean it. "You take really good care of me, Gage. You do."

He gives me a look that tells me he doesn't believe me, so I tick off the evidence on my fingers: "You won't let me be around inappropriate behavior; you make me do my homework; you sleep with me in the storage closet of Lighthouse even though you could have a bed on the boys' floor; you give me fashion tips . . ."

He looks at me when I say this, one eyebrow up. I can see a little smile on his lips.

I move to a new finger. "You came back to make sure I was OK even though you knew you might get fired. You came back."

"Always, B'Neatie," he says. "Always."

· 27 ·
DETENTION SLIPS

I'm alone, sitting at a giant wooden table in the conference room, serving my detention. The room has two doors — one right off the school office and the other off the hall. I keep my head lowered, focused on my report, so I don't see the kids who pass by the doors on their way home, and so I can pretend they don't see me.

Yesterday at Briggs's, I copied down a few of my favorite Louisa May Alcott quotes, which I'm hoping to use in my paper somewhere. There's one quote in particular that I keep reading over and over again:

What do girls do who haven't any mothers to help them through their troubles?

And I want to say, yeah, what *do* such girls do? Please tell me! What would my mother say about my slippery slide from being a shiny gifted student to one who has to serve detention? One whose teachers and even her best friend seem to have given up on?

I'm rereading the other quotes to see how I might work them into my paper when Daniel slips in through the hall door.

I glance around, hoping he wasn't seen. "Haven't you already done detention?"

He nods as he plunks down into a seat. "You wouldn't talk to me in class."

"You kept talking when we weren't supposed to. And now you're talking to me here and you're not supposed to. You're going to get us both in trouble," I say. *"Again."*

"Hey." He taps his fingers lightly on the table. "You're the one who wanted a secret spring blizzard, remember?"

He has a point. And he's kind enough not to mention that it was my glitter that caused the most problems.

I give a long sigh. "I guess it doesn't matter now

if I get in trouble again," I say, leaning back in my chair. "This detention has probably sealed my fate, as Mademoiselle Barbary likes to say. And that fate doesn't include Carter."

"Why does Carter matter so much to you anyway? It's not so much better than Wilson."

"Lots of reasons," I say.

"Tell me one."

"My mother wanted me to go there. It was basically her dying wish."

Daniel looks at me sympathetically. After a long silence, he says softly, "But why do *you* want to go there?"

I open my mouth, expecting the answer to be right there, on the tip of my tongue. But nothing comes out. I close my mouth and think about it— really think about it.

"I've lost a lot of things in my life," I say slowly. "Right now, I still have Eastland Elementary. I belong here. But after that . . ."

I pause for a moment, trying to gather my thoughts. "To me, Carter feels like a place where I could belong. It's where everyone in my family went—Mama and Dad, Gage, even Janna. It's a part of my history, but it's also my future." I shrug, feeling suddenly self-conscious. "Anyway, that's why I want to go to Carter."

Daniel is smiling, and I think he's going to make fun of me. But instead he says, "And that's why you care about the Eastland traditions."

He's right. I never did work up the courage to say as much to Mr. Chandler, but to me, the Eastland Elementary traditions aren't just about getting to stop work to cut paper or wearing funny hats. They're also about feeling like you belong somewhere. That you're part of a shared history, part of a family.

"So, when do you want to do Crazy Hat Day?" Daniel asks.

I laugh. Somehow I don't think Mr. Chandler intended for us to hatch our next plot while sitting in detention. But what do I have to lose at this point, really? I've already got one detention on my record. And if it's too late for me to get into Carter, at least it's not too late for me to revive another of my favorite Eastland traditions.

Together, Daniel and I make a plan for the next step of our campaign. Then, just as we're leaving, I point to another Louisa May Alcott quote from my notes. "This one makes me think of you," I tell Daniel shyly.

He reads it silently:

A faithful friend is a strong defense; And he that hath found him hath found a treasure.

And when he smiles, it really is like finding a treasure.

· 28 ·
FORMS

After I've served my detention, I take the bus to the Port City library, where Gage is going to pick me up. (I'm not supposed to go back to Head Start until I've been free of the flu for two more days.) When I get to the library, I find a carrel and pull out my application to Carter. On our way out of the school, Daniel had persuaded me that I should still at least apply. "It doesn't cost you anything," he'd said, and I wondered how much he knew about my situation. "And the worst that could happen is that you don't get in—which is what will *definitely* happen if you don't even bother to apply."

He had some good points.

There they are again—those spaces on the application that demand an address. I suppose I could write in Briggs's address, but that might get him in trouble. I could put down Chloe's address, but what if Gage and Chloe break up? I'm worried about that. We haven't seen much of Chloe lately—not since Gage got his job at Jiffy Lube. I wonder if they had a fight or if Gage is too proud to crash with her now that he should be able to afford a place of his own.

I could write in Janna's address, but the last thing I want is my acceptance or rejection letter being sent to Janna's place. She'd want to know why I used her address instead of Briggs's—which she thinks is our address. And that's assuming she'd even bother letting me know that a letter came in the first place.

We need an apartment! That's all there is to it. We need to figure this out!

I look up at the clock on the wall. I still have an hour before Gage gets here. I walk up to Mrs. Getchel at the front desk and ask her for the address of the Housing Authority.

"The Housing Authority, dear?"

I nod. She doesn't say anything else. That's the

great thing about librarians; they'll help you find information without being too nosy. She writes the address down on a scrap of paper, and right away I recognize the street. It's quite far from here, in one of the really pretty neighborhoods, which seems a little inconsiderate. Not only do most of the people who need to fill out forms with the Housing Authority likely need to pay to take the bus there, but then they have to pass by a bunch of beautiful homes that they'll never be able to afford. Why not place the Housing Authority office closer to the shelters?

"Is there anything else I can help you with, dear?" Mrs. Getchel asks in a very kind voice.

I decide to be brave. "I need some housing forms so my family can get a voucher," I say. "But I don't have the time or the money to go all the way to the other side of the city."

She thinks for a moment. "Perhaps the forms are online."

Why didn't I think of that?

"Do you want me to help you look?"

"That's OK," I say. "If they're online, I can find them."

It costs twenty-five cents per page to use the printer at the library. I hope the forms are short.

There is a lot to read on the Housing Authority site, and it looks like there's maybe even more than one program that Gage and I qualify for. They all have a waiting period, though, so they recommend applying to more than one at the same time. There's a faster program that would help us if we were living in the shelter, but unfortunately, living in the shelter isn't an option for us.

I've just finished reading all of the information and have pulled up the voucher application form when Gage walks up behind me.

"What are you doing, B'Neatie?"

"I found the Housing Authority forms!"

Gage looks over my shoulder and frowns. "Didn't I tell you that I would take care of that?"

"Yeah, but I thought—"

"Come on," he says. He turns and walks back out through the double doors.

I click out of the page, grab my backpack, and race after him. "Wait up, Gage!" I yell as soon as I'm on the street.

He turns and faces me. "Don't you think I want an apartment, too? Don't you think that I am just as tired as you are of never knowing where I'm going to sleep each night? Don't you think I'm doing everything I possibly can?"

He starts walking — to where, I don't even know.

"I was just trying to help!" I shout.

No response.

"I was just trying to help, Gage!"

And I realize, as soon as the words are out of my mouth, that those are the same words Janna used all the time. "I'm just trying to help, Gage."

Gage *hated* Janna's help and told her he didn't need it, but she never stopped trying to give it to him. Maybe Gage resented the implication that he couldn't handle things on his own. Or maybe accepting Janna's help made Gage feel disloyal to Mama.

I never did understand why Janna and Gage couldn't seem to get along, why they were like two stubborn elk, butting heads and locking horns over every little thing. But as I walk behind Gage, I think back on the pictures in Janna's scrapbook. I think of the big secret I uncovered, of our dad dating Janna before he married Mama. I wonder if Gage knew all about that. I wonder what else Gage knows that I don't.

It turns out that we're going to Chloe's, which makes me happy. And once we're on the bus, Gage has cooled down, which also makes me happy. By the time we reach Chloe's house, he's back to being his old self. When we enter the building, he pauses to slip out of his Jiffy Lube jumpsuit and put on some deodorant.

"Can I use some, too?" I ask apprehensively.

He starts to laugh but stops himself. "Sure," he says, handing it over. "But you'll smell like me."

"Then maybe Chloe will fall in love with me, too," I tease, struggling a little to apply the deodorant with my shirt still on.

Gage shakes his head. "Come on, dork," he says, climbing the stairs to her apartment. "You don't need deodorant to get Chloe to love you. She already does. But we'll see about getting you some of your own."

Nate answers the door. "Hey, guys," he says. "Chloe! Company!" he calls over his shoulder.

Chloe's sitting on a bar stool in the kitchen. Next to her is a guy I've never seen before.

"Hey," Chloe says, jumping down from her stool and running to hug Gage. "Did we make plans?" she asks, looking confused.

"No, I just miss you." Gage looks over at the guy in the kitchen. "Thought I'd see if I could take you out for dinner."

"Tonight?" she asks.

Gage's face falls, and I'm sure mine does, too. "Yeah, tonight. You got plans?"

She nods reluctantly. "Wyatt and I are working on a project tonight," she says, gesturing toward the mystery man.

"Due tomorrow," Wyatt adds.

"You don't have time to stop for dinner?" Gage asks. But he and I both know that we didn't come here just for dinner. And I think Chloe knows it, too.

"I'm sorry, babe. We were just going to order in and work through the night. But you guys are welcome to stay if you want."

"Nah, we'd just be in the way," says Gage. "We'll peace. Come on, Ari."

Chloe gives Gage a kiss, but he pulls away after only a second. And just like that, we're back on the streets.

"Where to next?" I ask. "Briggs's?"

Gage doesn't say anything. His sour mood is back.

"Briggs's?" I say louder.

Gage shakes his head no. "His landlord has him freaked out."

"Perry and Kristen's?" I'm trying to keep up with Gage.

"I don't know what's up with Perry. He hasn't answered my calls for a few days." Gage slows down. "How about Sasha? Do you think you could stay with her tonight?"

I start to say no—Sasha's hardly talked to me in forever—but maybe I could tell her everything tonight. Maybe that would help get us back to being best friends.

"Do you want to call her?" Gage asks.

Feeling full of wishfulness, I take the phone.

Marianna answers. "Why, Ari," she says, "don't you have Sasha's new cell number? Or do old habits simply die hard? Hold on—I'll get her."

"Hey, Ari," Sasha says a few moments later. "What's up?" But there's no happiness in her voice. It's like she's a balloon and all the air has been sucked out of her. I feel my wishfulness start to fade.

"Can I come over tonight?" I say. "It would be fun to catch up, and I have something important to tell you."

"Can it wait? I have lots of homework. Plus, my mother is making me finish the Carter application."

"We could do it together!" I say. "I only just started filling out mine."

There is a long silence on the phone.

"Um, I don't think so. Keisha and I had a long talk today, Ari, and well, she thinks—and I guess I agree—that you've become kind of weird lately. You never invite me over to Janna's anymore, and you're always hanging out with Daniel. I mean, you didn't even tell me about the snowflakes thing! What kind of a friend does that? So I've been thinking that maybe we need to make other friends. Especially since we're about to go off to different middle schools."

Different middle schools. The words are like daggers.

I can feel Gage looking at me, and I turn away, blinking back tears.

"Anyway, I'm glad you called. I've been wanting to get this off my chest for a while, but you kept ignoring my messages."

Messages I never got because the only number Sasha knew to call was Janna's. But it's too late to try to explain things now. She has already broken up with me.

"Yeah, OK," I say, and hang up. No doubt Sasha and Keisha will be dissecting this call tomorrow, discussing how I didn't even say good-bye.

I turn back to Gage and shake my head, handing him the phone.

Gage doesn't say anything. We walk together in silence, the light growing dim around us.

"Let's get to the soup kitchen," he says, "before it closes."

I don't even bother to nod. I've already gone invisible.

· 29 ·
COMICS

Fortunately, the line outside the soup kitchen isn't long. I'm standing behind Gage, waiting to enter the basement of the stone church and thinking about the first question on the Carter application: *How would other people describe you?* Holy moly, what a question! It seems to me that it would depend on who the other person was. I try to think of one-word answers that people I know might give:

Gage: *persistent*

Mademoiselle: *disappointing*

Ms. Finch: *sneaky*

Mr. O.: I'm not sure. Two weeks ago he might have said *irresponsible.* But if I turn in my rough draft tomorrow—and if we stay at Lighthouse tonight, I should be able to finish it—he might change his word to *hardworking*.

Mr. Chandler: *delinquent*

Sasha: That one's easy. *Weird*

Daniel:

I'm trying to carefully choose my word for Daniel when suddenly something or someone barrels into my legs. I nearly fall over.

It's Omar!

"Where. Have. You. Been?" he demands.

I'd forgotten that Omar's family sometimes comes here to the soup kitchen. "I was sick," I tell him. "I have to make sure that I'm all better before coming back to Head Start."

Gage, who has been busy texting someone—Chloe, I imagine, or maybe Perry or Briggs—turns around just as Omar's mother comes up the line to get her son.

"Sorry about that, Ari," she says. "He's been asking about you every single day. We told you were sick, but I think he was afraid you'd disappeared!"

"Oh, it's no problem," I say. "I've missed him, too! But I should be back soon," I promise Omar.

Omar and his mother move back in line to where his dad was holding a spot, while Gage and I pass through the doorway. Inside, the line continues to weave along the wall until it reaches the serving table. Already, many of the tables in the center of the room are filled with people gobbling down their warm meal. I try to see what's on their plates tonight, but I'm not close enough yet.

I think about Omar as we meander closer and wonder if he and his family are living at the family shelter—or perhaps one of the long-term motels. Chloe's roommate Cody once suggested to Gage that we rent a motel room, but Gage said that you end up paying so much money for rent and fast food (most motels only have a microwave in the room, if that) that it's nearly impossible to save enough money to move out of it.

Good smells are coming from the kitchen, and word has passed back to us that tonight's dinner is beef-vegetable soup, bread, corn dogs, salad, and dessert.

"What kind of dessert?" I hear Omar say from somewhere behind me.

I smile and shuffle forward with the line, almost as excited as Omar about tonight's menu. The earlier tension between me and Gage has eased with time, and even the sting of Chloe's rejection has dulled. Maybe tonight won't be such a bad night after all.

And that's when I see her. Standing at the back of the room, ladling out soup to the masses, is Keisha. As in Sasha's new best friend, Keisha. Volunteering at the soup kitchen on the exact night when Gage and I decide to come by.

"I'm not hungry," I say to Gage, ducking behind him and hoping that Keisha hasn't already caught sight of me.

"What?" Gage says somewhat loudly.

"I don't feel good. I'll wait outside."

"Do you want me to come with you?"

I peek around Gage's shoulder. Keisha's dad is looking over, but Keisha is busy portioning out soup.

I shake my head. "I think I just need to get some fresh air," I say. "Can you get me a plate, though? I changed my mind about not being hungry," I say, and then hightail it out of there without waiting for an answer.

On the street, I bump into Reggie and Amelia. "Hey, Ari," he says. "Coming to dinner?"

"My brother is getting me food," I say. "I needed some fresh air. I've been under the weather lately," I add, which isn't really a lie. "Would you like me to watch Amelia while you eat?"

"If you're sure you don't mind," Reggie says. "I bet Amelia would like that."

Reggie pulls a leash from his backpack. I take it from him, intending to walk Amelia up and down the block a few times, but I don't get far, because people keep stopping us. I'm amazed at how many folks on the way to the soup kitchen recognize her, want to give her a pat. An older woman and a boy about my age have both saved dog treats—the kinds that you can get for free at the bookstore or the coffee shop—for Amelia.

It's getting cold and I'm beginning to see my breath when Reggie comes back and tells me that Gage is waiting for me on the steps of Lighthouse.

"I hope you're hungry, because he's got quite a plate of food for you!"

I *am* pretty hungry, I realize. "Thanks for letting me walk Amelia," I say, patting her on the head one last time, reluctant to leave her side. Also, a small part of me is hoping that Reggie might ask if we want to stay in his storage unit tonight.

"I'm the one doing the thanking here," he says, smiling broadly. Just then, a young couple with a little baby approach us.

"Reggie!" the woman says, hugging him warmly. The man shakes Reggie's hand while the baby gurgles at Amelia.

"Mary, Travis, I'd like you to meet my friend Ari. Ari, this is Mary, Travis, and their daughter, Sarah."

"Nice to meet you," I say, feeling suddenly shy, like I'm a third wheel. I should have known that lots of people would know Reggie, too, if so many people knew Amelia. But somehow I guess I'd thought that he was my secret.

"Thanks again, Ari," Reggie says, and he walks

off with the small family. As they go, I hear Reggie say, "It's not the Taj Mahal, but it's warm. . . ."

And I realize that just as Reggie isn't my secret, neither is his little home. I picture the family of three all warm and snuggly there—probably with Amelia, too.

Gage is right where Reggie said he'd be. He's spread out on the top step of Lighthouse—a bowl of soup on each side of him and a takeout bag in his lap. He lifts up one of the bowls and I plunk down beside him.

"That girl serving tonight—she someone you know?" he asks.

I nod. "Keisha. Sasha's new BFF. Do you think she saw me?"

"I doubt it. You ducked out of there pretty quick, and she wasn't really looking at the faces of the people in line."

I sure hope Gage is right. The last thing I need is for word to get out that I eat at the soup kitchen. People would start asking uncomfortable questions, and it would probably be just a matter of time till someone thought to check in with Janna. Not to mention the fun Keisha, Linnie, and Sasha would probably have gossiping about me being dirty, smelly, *and* someone who eats with the homeless.

West comes out when we're nearly done eating. "Hey, man," he says to Gage, and they do some elaborate handshake thing. "Hey, Ari," he says to me.

"Hi, West," I say around my last bite of apple pie.

"Listen, Gage . . ." he begins, sounding a little nervous, which of course makes me nervous, too. Is he going to tell us that we can't stay here tonight?

"What's up?" Gage asks, and I can tell that he's trying hard to sound nonchalant.

"There's a new supervisor on tonight," West says. "I don't think I can sneak you into the storage area with him on watch. You'll have to register."

"But Ari isn't old enough, remember?" says Gage.

"I'll leave her age blank when I fill out the paperwork," says West. "It will look like an oversight."

I frown. "Gage and I will have to sleep in separate rooms?"

West nods. "You'll be OK, Ari. The girls who come here in the middle of the week are typically well behaved. They know they'll be asked to leave if they're not."

"But what if someone under eighteen wants Gage's bed?" That's the rule at Lighthouse; anyone between eighteen and twenty has to give up his or her bed if a minor needs it.

"Then he'll have to give it up," West says. "But if I know Gage, he'll figure something out and be back for you in the morning."

I look at Gage. He looks so tired. Like he can't take one more step tonight. "It'll be OK," he says. "It's only one night. If it comes to it, I'll just crash at Chloe's place."

I hold his gaze, trying to see if he's lying to make me feel better, but I can't tell.

I shrug. What choice do I really have?

I gather up our trash and follow the guys inside. Gage goes into West's office to check us in. I'm left in the living room with a group of five teenagers: two girls and three boys. I sit down at the table that's off to the side and try to become invisible.

As I wait for Gage to be done, I think again of Keisha and of how she and Sasha seem to have become best friends in no time flat. How was it possible that Sasha could ditch me so quickly and become best friends with someone she'd barely spoken to till a few weeks ago?

I'm reminded of a math game we played in third grade called Mingle. We'd all stand and buzz around one another like bees, mumbling; "Mingle, mingle, mingle." Then, when our teacher called out a number, we had to quickly form ourselves into groups of that number. It was a way of explaining division and remainders. If you weren't fast at grabbing friends, if you didn't get into a group of two, or three, or four, you were a remainder.

Now that school's nearly over, there seems to be a game of Mingle going on. Kids know who will likely go to Carter, to Saint Anthony's, or to Wilson. They're grabbing one another and holding on, counting on an alliance when they get there. Sasha and Keisha have found one another; Catherine McCauley, another girl headed to Saint Anthony's, has grabbed onto Linnie. But I don't have anyone. Right now, I'm a remainder.

• • •

Eventually Gage and West come out of the office, and it's time for us to find beds on our separate floors. I want to ask West if there's really a bed for Gage or if they're just going through the motions for my benefit, but I don't dare. Besides, I'm not sure I want to know the answer.

West and Gage stay behind on the second floor, and I give Gage a quick hug before I turn to head up to the girls' floor. "I'll meet you in the kitchen at seven for breakfast, B'Neatie," Gage calls after me.

I nod but don't turn back. I'm afraid he'll take one look at my face and know how scared I am to sleep on the third floor without him in a room full of strange girls.

Even though there can't be more than seven girls in the room—the maximum is eight, and West assured me there was a bed for me—it sounds like there are about twenty girls in there. I enter the room slowly, taking in as much as possible as quickly as possible and trying to find an empty bed.

"Hey, there!" one of the girls says, spotting me. She's blond and pretty, maybe a few years younger than Gage. But definitely older than me. Most of the girls are a lot older than me, I notice. The next-youngest girl seems to be about fourteen, and she's sitting on a bed with two older girls who look just like her. Sisters, I bet.

"Hi," I say quietly, making my way over to a bed that seems to be empty. I set my backpack down on it cautiously, half expecting someone to yell at me and tell me I'm taking her spot. But no one does.

"You here by yourself?" the blond girl asks.

I shake my head. "My brother is on the boys' floor. He's eighteen," I add, somehow feeling a bit safer for having said this.

The girl nods. "Well, if you need anything, just ask. I'm Cassie. I'm here most nights, so I know the ropes. This here is Delia, and that over there is Jordanna. And those are the O'Riley sisters."

The other girls mumble greetings, and I relax a little, settling back on my bed and opening my backpack. This isn't so bad. If I can tune out the sound of the girls' chatter, I might even be able to finish my report before lights-out, which is at ten.

I'm scribbling away in my notebook and flipping through the pages of *Little Women* when the

273

youngest O'Riley sister comes over to my bed. I look up at her and smile, not wanting to seem unfriendly, but then I look back down at my book, hoping it's clear that I'm trying to work. But the girl just stands there, not saying anything. I try to ignore her, but it's hard to concentrate with her hovering in front of me. What does she want, anyway?

"What's that?" she asks.

I look up again. She's pointing at my Paper Things folder, which I took out of my backpack to get to my report. A few pieces of furniture and two of the people — a teenage boy named Alex and the toddler in the snowflake sweater, who doesn't have a name yet — peek out from the sides of the folder.

"Oh, nothing," I say, opening the folder a crack and sliding the clippings back inside.

I've barely closed it again when the girl snatches it up.

"Hey!" I say, reaching for it. But she turns so that it's too far away.

"Cool!" she says, flipping through the folder. "Are these, like, paper dolls or something?"

Her sisters gather around to see what it is

she's found, and soon Cassie and Jordanna come over, too.

I stand up and try to grab the folder back, but the girls block my way.

"What *is* all this stuff?" Cassie asks, laughing.

Now they're picking out their favorites and passing them around. My heart feels like it's lodged in my throat. "Please give them back," I say. But my voice is a squeak.

"What happened to him?" says Delia, holding Miles so everyone can see. "The adventures of Tape Man," she says, flying him around like he's a superhero or something.

I want to scream, "Give him back!" but I know this will only make them all more curious. So I smile like a stupid mannequin. . . .

"Look!" says one of the O'Riley sisters. She's drawn earrings on one of my teens, long dangly earrings.

The girls laugh, and suddenly everyone seems to have a pen. "I'll take her!" someone says, and grabs Natalie. "Ooh, give me him!" another girl says, snatching Alex from the pile. Soon everyone is doodling on my Paper Things, adding eyeglasses, tattoos, earrings, and other things that I can't bear to think about.

Hot tears burn my eyes. *Gage! Where's Gage?* I want to scream out his name, like a little kid would cry *Mom!* But he's not here—and even if he were, it's too late for him to do anything. My Paper Things are already ruined.

"Hey, kid, don't look so grim," Cassie says to me. "We're just having a little fun."

She hands me the people she's defaced—Mandy and Tamara and even little Nicky—and the other girls follow suit until I have everything back. Clearly the fun has worn off for them.

I stuff my Paper Things back into my folder numbly, trying not to look too closely at any of them. Four years of collecting and imagining and caring. Gone. Just like that.

I shove the folder in my backpack along with my unfinished report and my notebook and climb into bed, not even bothering to take off my uniform. Lights-out isn't for another half hour, but I don't care.

Right now, I don't care about anything.

· 30 ·
DOLLAR BILLS

I stay awake for hours, listening to the sounds of
the other girls in the room. They don't seem like
bad girls, I think dimly as their conversations wash
over me. They talk about school and boys and which
shelters have the comfiest beds or the best break-
fasts. They probably didn't mean any harm when
they drew all over my Paper Things, and it wasn't
exactly like I was shouting at them to stop.

But whether they meant harm or not, they had
no right to do what they did, and I can't help thinking that I hate each and every one of them.

Eventually, my eyes get heavy and I drift off to
sleep. But it's a light sleep, and that turns out to

be a good thing, because suddenly in the darkness I hear Gage's voice. At first I think I'm dreaming, but then the actual words penetrate—just barely distinguishable through the thin walls.

"My sister is upstairs," Gage says to someone. "Can you make sure someone tells her?"

I bolt awake, grab my backpack, and fly down the stairs. Gage is opening the front door when I call out his name.

"Ari!" he says, then quickly lowers his voice. "What are you doing up?"

"I heard you talking," I say, slipping my backpack onto my shoulders. "I figured you were leaving."

"Yeah, the room filled up. But I thought we agreed you'd stay here?"

I give him a look that says, *Don't even try to talk me into staying.*

"Grab that blanket," he says, pointing to one that has been unfolded on the couch.

I nab it and we're out the door. The night is frigid, and within minutes I can't feel my feet, but I know better than to complain. Besides, I am too tired to do much more than follow Gage up the hilly roads. This time he doesn't race ahead of me. He holds out his hand, and I take it.

At this hour, the city is much darker than I have ever seen it before. I look up as we walk and see stars. With the stars overhead and Gage's warm hand holding mine, I feel safe and protected and I know that everything will turn out OK.

Soon I realize that we're headed toward Chloe's. Just as I'm starting to worry that she might be upset to have us knock on her door in the middle of the night, we stop in front of her forest-green car.

"Where are we going?" I start to ask, wondering when Chloe gave Gage her car keys. But Gage doesn't answer. Instead, he takes a long, thin piece of metal from his back pocket and uses it to unlock the car door.

"Thank goodness her car is so old," Gage says as he opens the driver's-side door. "You can't do this on new cars. They've got computer systems and alarms."

I stare at the open door, still trying to make sense of what's happening.

"C'mon," Gage says, motioning for me to get in

and crawl over to the passenger side. "You're letting all the cold air in!"

As I slide into the seat, I think about the kid Chloe pays to protect this car. I sure hope he's sleeping right now.

I'm expecting Gage to do something to the ignition and drive us somewhere — Briggs's place, maybe, or Perry and Kristen's — but instead, he reclines his seat as far back as it'll go and settles in. And I finally get it. We're sleeping in Chloe's car.

I recline my seat, too, and cover up with the blanket. I'm cold to my bones and worry that Gage must be even colder without a blanket. But without a key, it's impossible to turn the heat on.

I try to share the blanket.

"Nah, I don't need it. Let me teach you a trick," he says. "Close your eyes and picture a little candle in your belly."

I look at him like he's crazy, but he just nods. "Go on, do it."

Slowly, I let my eyes droop closed and then think of a candle in my belly, just like he said.

"Concentrate on the flame," he says, his voice soft and warm in the cold, dark air. "Imagine the flame growing bigger, stronger. Feel the heat move from your belly to other parts of your body. Down your arms and legs, into your hands and feet. Now feel it moving up your neck and warming your face."

I do what he says, and holy moly, it actually works! I *do* feel warmer, like a little flame is moving through my body. I only shiver when I stop concentrating.

Between the late hour and the fact that we just walked across half the city, you would think that Gage and I would fall right to sleep, but neither of us does. We stare up at the sky through the moon roof of the car. I wonder what Gage is thinking— if he's wishing he weren't so full of pride that he could just go and knock on Chloe's door, or if he's upset at having to give up his bed at Lighthouse for some stranger.

My own thoughts swirl around, drifting from my ruined Paper Things to Sasha and Keisha and Linnie and on to Daniel and the Eastland traditions and Carter. Eventually, though, they settle on one thought, and I find myself speaking in the dark.

"Did you know that Dad dated Janna before he married Mama?" I ask Gage, my voice sounding loud in the silent night.

"What? No way," he says. "What makes you think *that*?"

I tell him about Janna's scrapbook, about the pictures of Janna and our dad.

"How do you know it was Dad? You never even met him."

"It *was*, Gage," I say. "It was the same man as in Mama's wedding pictures. It was someone who looked exactly like you."

"Weird," he says, though I can tell that he doesn't fully believe me. I can't really blame him; I saw the pictures, and I can still hardly believe it myself.

And then something occurs to me, something that feels so right that I wonder if this was why my brain was fixating on those pictures. "Maybe some of Janna's grouchiness, some of her having to be better than Mama, has more to do with Dad than with you."

Gage grunts, but I can practically feel the wheels in his head working away, turning over this new information and trying to make sense of it.

After that, he's quiet for a while — so quiet that I wonder if he's fallen asleep. But then he speaks up. "I know you're looking forward to us having our own place, and I am, too. But West was telling me about this group house that we might be able to move into. It's called a stability house, and you pay only a small amount of rent, with the rest of your money going into a savings account to help pay for a future apartment. And the program lets you take classes or even attend college so you can find an even better job."

I haven't heard Gage this excited since he got his job at Jiffy Lube.

"Who else would live in the house?" I ask.

"The family house is filled right now, but they're trying to put together a new house with eighteen- to twenty-two-year-olds."

"But I'm only—"

"West is working on getting you a room in the house, too."

I think about living in a house like that. It

wouldn't be like having a real apartment, one you can decorate, one where you can spread out your things and leave them, one where you can stand in front of an open refrigerator door and know that all the food inside is yours for the taking. I'm not even sure you'd have privacy. The stability house sort of sounds like the shelter, only there would be the same people every night.

I think of the girls back at Lighthouse and my folder of ruined Paper Things.

"It sure would solve a lot of problems," Gage says.

I want to be as excited as Gage sounds, to reassure him that I'll be happy anywhere as long as we're together. But I'm filled with doubts and fears. "What will I do on nights when you want to go on a date with Chloe?" I ask. "Will I stay at the house by myself? And what will I tell my friends? I can't exactly invite them for sleepovers at a group home."

Not that I have any friends anymore, I think. And maybe Gage thinks that, too, but he's nice enough not to say anything.

"We'll cross that bridge when we come to it. *If* we come to it." Gage sighs. "But it sure would help things if Chloe could stop thinking of me as homeless."

I raise myself up on my elbows. "You're not—
we're not homeless," I say.

But Gage is quiet. So I say it again: "We're not
homeless."

"Think about it, Ari. What does it mean to be
homeless?"

I think of the people that I pass on the streets,
the ones who are huddled against buildings or standing on curbs, asking for money, sometimes talking
to themselves. *They're* homeless. I think of the girls
at Lighthouse who drew all over my Paper Things
and talked about which shelters had the nicest beds.
They're homeless, too. But then I think of Reggie,
and Omar, and the young family with the baby.

"Homeless people are people who don't have
homes," I say slowly.

"Right," says Gage.

Like us, I realize.

31

GIFT WRAP

In the morning, before the bell for homeroom, I do something I've never done before. I sneak into the cafeteria for free breakfast. Janna always insisted that we start the day with a good breakfast, even when Gage swore that he wasn't hungry, that his stomach didn't want a thing. And then, when we were living with friends, I'd eat whatever they ate for breakfast: Cheerios at Briggs's, frozen waffles at Chloe's. Lighthouse gives the kids granola bars and juice in the morning. But this morning I've had nothing, and I'm starving.

The hardest part turns out not to be getting the food. Apparently, at breakfast no one checks to see if you're signed up—or if you're even approved. It's easy for me to slide in and take a tray with scrambled eggs and home-fried potatoes.

The hardest part is figuring out where to sit. I look around the room and realize that I've never thought about who comes to the cafeteria before school starts. Given that we all have this one thing in common, I should feel relaxed and friendly, able to sit with whoever catches my eye. But instead, I feel oddly shy and embarrassed, like everyone in this room knows that I'm not really supposed to be here and resents me for it.

I sit down at the end of one table, close enough to some kids that I don't feel like I'm all alone, but far enough away that I don't invade their space. Then I open up one of my Louisa May Alcott books and start to read, even though I've read every page of this book already. I notice then that the book is overdue and realize I'll have to raid my piggy bank at Briggs's place to pay the fine.

Gage and I left the car just as the sun was rising this morning—partly because we were so cold and needed to move around, and partly because Gage was afraid Chloe would catch him in her car—so after breakfast I still have plenty of time to go to the girls' room to freshen up. I go into the handicap stall and change into a clean shirt and uniform, rolling up the stuff I wore last night and cramming it into my bag. It's smelly and hopelessly wrinkled already, so a few more wrinkles won't hurt it.

I head to the sink to wash my face and maybe sneak in a quick sponge bath of my underarms with wet paper towels. When I look in the mirror and see my reflection, I groan. I have dark circles under my eyes, and my hair's a mess. I can just imagine what Sasha and Keisha are going to say about *that*.

Just then, someone else slips into the bathroom. It's a girl from my class that I recognize, though we hardly ever speak.

"Hey, Hannah," I say, turning on the water and washing my hands like I just used the toilet.

"Hey, Ari," she says, then yawns hugely. "Oops, sorry!" she apologizes, laughing.

I keep the water running while she uses the toilet, washing my face as quickly as I can, hoping to finish before she comes out and sees me. I don't dare wash my underarms, though; thankfully a quick whiff assures me that they're not too bad today. Not yet, anyway.

Hannah comes out of her stall while I'm patting my face dry with paper towels. I'm about to toss them in the trash can and hurry away when she says to me, "You know how to braid, right?"

I feel heat rising from my belly to the tip of my ears. Her tone may not be as nasty as Keisha's, but I can tell that what she's really saying is *Why don't you braid your hair instead of letting it tangle into a total rat's nest?*

"You used to have the coolest braids," she says, coming up to the sink next to me and washing her hands. "Do you think you could braid my hair this morning? I have a comb and a bunch of elastics in my backpack."

I try to hide my surprise. "I'm not very good at it," I admit. "Jan—someone else used to braid my hair, but I can try."

I stand behind her and carefully comb the snags out of her hair, relieved to know that I'm not the only girl at Eastland Elementary with snarls. I gather her hair into sections and try my best to make straight parts. It turns out that braiding someone else's hair is *très* easier than trying to braid your own, and I'm pretty happy with the results. I can tell by Hannah's smile that she's happy, too.

"Thanks!" she says. "My mom used to do my hair in the mornings, but ever since she switched to the night shift, she's usually asleep when I leave for school."

"I know what you mean," I say. "Janna hasn't been around lately to do my hair, either." This is one of those statements that's not really a lie but isn't exactly the truth either. But I want Hannah to know that I understand what it's like not to have a mom around to do things for you.

"Would you like me to try to do yours?" Hannah asks. "I'll warn you, though: I don't have a lot of experience." She smiles again, and it's contagious.

"That's OK," I say, grinning and turning around. "I can walk you through the trickiest bits."

And then, for some unknown reason, I tell her, "I had breakfast here this morning. It wasn't half bad."

• • •

After announcements, Mr. O. tells us that the fifth-grade teachers had their grade-level meeting yesterday. We know what's coming. Some of us sit up straighter, which is pretty funny. Do we think that our good posture will make our names magically appear on Mr. O.'s list of students who got leadership roles? I look around the room, trying to determine who has yet to be patrol leader—the role I really, really, really want, though I'd take any job offered to me right now.

This is the last time that these announcements will be made this year.

Mr. O. announces the library helper. It's Matthew Stone. He pumps his fist and then relaxes back into his chair.

Some of the kids sitting up straight won't even be applying to Carter. But maybe there are other reasons for wanting to be patrol leader. Janna always seemed to know when the new leadership roles were announced. I wouldn't be in the house for more than a few minutes when she'd ask, "Who's patrol leader next month?" I felt bad when I admitted that I hadn't been chosen, like I was letting her down. Maybe others, like me, are hoping to avoid that same old question in the same old way.

I don't think Gage thinks about me and leadership roles. I don't think he realizes how hard it is to get into Carter. I think he just assumes that I'm smart, so I'll go.

Joya and Ellison are chosen as math tutors, which seems especially unfair, since I've often been asked to show them how to do something in math.

I guess I'm not as smart as we thought I was. Or maybe I'm not as smart as I used to be.

Sunjay and Thalia are patrol leaders. The last patrol leaders of the year. Fifth grade is almost over, and I will never, ever, ever be a patrol leader.

Never.

Makes me glad that I don't have a scrapbook.

In social studies class, kids who are finished with their reports early (thank goodness they aren't officially due until next week) are giving presentations on their famous nineteenth-century Americans. Linnie shows us a poster she made about Davy Crockett, who was known as "the king of the wild frontier." Next, Sunjay tells us about a man who lived more than a hundred years ago named Henry David Thoreau. I sit up taller in my chair to listen when I hear that Henry David Thoreau was a friend of Louisa May Alcott's! He was also an author, but Sunjay is talking about how he believed in something called civil disobedience. I repeat the words in my head, trying to puzzle out the meaning, but I don't think I quite get it. When Sunjay asks, "Are there any questions?" I raise my hand tentatively and say, "What exactly is 'civil disobedience'?"

I hear Keisha snicker behind me, but I try to ignore her. I bet she doesn't really know what it means either.

"Good question, Arianna," Mr. O. says, and I'm glad I asked it. "Sunjay?"

"'Civil disobedience' is when someone breaks a law to make a point," Sunjay says, and you can tell that he knows a lot about it. "Henry David Thoreau didn't pay his taxes because he didn't believe in slavery and he didn't support the Mexican-American War. Back then, part of everyone's tax money went to fund both of those things, so by not paying his taxes, Thoreau was sending a message."

"I'm going to refuse to do homework because I don't believe in it," Joey says.

"Does it have to be a law?" I ask, ignoring Joey. "Is it civil disobedience if you break a rule?"

"Like when you hang snowflakes even though your principal has abolished the Eastland tradition?" says Mr. O. He smiles right at me.

I smile back. One proud moment lifted from my sack. "Or wear a crazy hat to protest the loss of traditions."

"We should do that!" Keisha says. "We should all wear crazy hats on the same day to let Mr. Chandler know that we believe in our traditions! It could be an act of civil disobedience."

I open my mouth to say that I am already planning to do that, that I need to organize it so that I can put it on my Carter application. But everyone is too busy talking excitedly about the secret Crazy Hat Day.

Just like that, I'm invisible.

• • •

The tiredness hits me after Mr. O.'s class and gets worse throughout the day. By the time my last class—computer lab—rolls around, I can hardly keep my eyes open.

Ms. Finch teaches us how to make multimedia presentations using animation, audio clips, and video clips. The stuff she shows us is actually *très* cool, and I might even be able to enhance my Louisa May Alcott presentation with clips from the movie version of *Little Women* or an animated slide show of the various places she and her family lived before settling in Concord, Massachusetts . . . if only I could focus.

"Ari, would you mind staying for a few minutes at the end of class?" Ms. Finch asks quietly as she walks by my workstation. My heart plummets. *Did I actually shut my eyes?* Is she still mad at me about sneaking into the lab that one time?

I'm wide awake for the rest of class, but now it's anxiety rather than tiredness that keeps me from focusing on the lesson. When the bell rings, I stand by the door and wait for everyone to leave. Daniel gives me a searching look, but I tell him that

I want to ask Ms. Finch something about today's lesson.

Thankfully, he doesn't offer to stick around. "OK. I'll see you tomorrow," he says, and heads off.

When it's just me and Ms. Finch in the room, she walks over to her desk and retrieves a paper bag from the bottom drawer. "I was thinking of you recently, Ari," she says, opening the bag.

I'm holding my breath, wondering where this is going.

"You see, I bought my niece a new pair of shoes, but they didn't fit her. I swear that girl grows six inches each time I see her! Anyway, you'll probably think I'm crazy for saying this—and I might be way off base—but for some reason they reminded me of you. If you like them and they fit, you're welcome to have them."

She pulls a pair of plaid Top-Siders from the bag. They are without a doubt the cutest pair of shoes I have ever seen in my whole life! She hands them to me.

I hold them in both my hands, aware that my mouth is hanging open but unable to close it. Ms.

Finch was giving me a free pair of shoes — of really *cute* shoes. Why me? Surely lots of girls in her classes might like these shoes and might be the right size for them. Was it because she'd noticed that my shoes were falling apart? Were these pity shoes? Or did she really mean it when she said they reminded her of me?

"Try them on," she says.

My fingers barely work as I pull off my old shoes, and I wonder if *everyone* has noticed how ratty they are. Slowly I slip one foot into the Top-Siders, then the other. I wiggle my toes around. They are the perfect size.

Maybe this is an act of charity, and maybe Gage would want me to say thanks but no thanks. But looking down at my feet in these brand-new, *très* cool shoes, I decide I don't care why Ms. Finch is giving them to me. I'm just grateful that she is.

And suddenly I'm crying.

"What's wrong, Ari?" she asks, her voice gentler than I've ever heard it before. "Why are you crying?"

"That's just what I do," I say, sniffling and smiling through my tears. "I cry when I'm happy. And these shoes make me very, very happy. Thank you, Ms. Finch."

Now it's Ms. Finch's turn to get a bit teary. "You're very welcome, Arianna."

"What should I . . . ? If someone asks . . . ?"

"Tell them a friend gave them to you," Ms. Finch says. "It's the truth."

I give her a big thank-you smile, then tuck my old shoes into my backpack. I turn to leave but stop myself. "I'm sorry about that day in your class, the day I was working on my bibliography."

"Oh," she says, brushing my words away. "I may have overreacted. I shouldn't have taken your actions so personally. I realized that after you left. That's why I passed your homework on to Mr. O'Neil."

It was Ms. Finch who turned it in?

I want to rush over and hug her, tell her that she saved my life, but before my new dazzling feet can move, she's behind her desk, glasses on, back to work.

I feel like Cinderella in my new shoes. During dismissal, kids tell me how cool they are and ask where I got them. *Tell them a friend gave them to you. It's the truth.* So that's what I do. I wish Sasha and I still did our partway walk home; I would have liked for her to see them. But I'll wear them tomorrow and every day after, so I suppose she'll see them soon enough.

My new shoes are also a big hit at Head Start. Juju keeps rubbing her hands on them like they're magic or something, and Carol tells me I look very fashion-forward.

The one person who *doesn't* love my new shoes is Gage.

"You could have used the money in your piggy bank to buy shoes," he says as we're walking to Chloe's. I think about my piggy bank and wonder how much money is in there. Would there really be enough for a new pair of shoes? I start daydreaming about all of the apartment stuff I could buy with that much money: silverware, towels, sheets . . .

"Anyway, *I* like them," I say to Gage, ignoring his bad mood. "And they'll keep my feet warmer than my old shoes."

Today the stairwell at Chloe's is crowded with a bunch of guys, spillover from some party happening in the apartment below hers. The strong scents of their shaving creams and hair gels cover the usual smell of pee.

"Hey," says a guy about Gage's age, but he doesn't say it to Gage—he says it to me. He takes a drink from a can of beer.

"Hi," I mutter, my eyes on the stairs in front of me.

"Hey, how old are you?" another guy asks as we climb the stairs.

"Don't answer," says Gage softly.

Chloe greets us in the doorway, seeming really excited to see us. Like usual, I slip inside the apartment to give them a moment. Neither Nate nor Cody is home. The apartment seems empty without them. I hear Gage say, "I want to, Chloe, but I can't. I don't want to leave Ari alone with those creeps downstairs."

"She doesn't need someone to watch her. She's old enough to *be* a babysitter, Gage. And it's not fair to keep asking me to pass things up or to go alone."

I hate that I'm the reason Chloe and Gage are fighting. I don't want them to break up. Gage is trying to come through for Chloe, to come through for me, to come through for Mama.

Stay together always. That's what Mama said. That was the promise. But I think that both Gage and I know deep down that it's not the promise that's making us hold on to each other so tightly.

It's the fear of letting go.

I can't hear what Gage is saying, but I know he's upset.

Quickly I step into the hall. "Sorry to interrupt," I say, "but I just remembered that Sasha invited me to stay at her place tonight. Would that be OK?"

Chloe looks at Gage, hopeful. But Gage frowns. "It's a school night," he says.

"I know," I say. "But Marianna said we can work on our Carter applications together. I could really use the help."

"Gage . . ." Chloe pleads. I try not to feel hurt by how badly she wants me out of their hair.

"Chloe and I could have plans tonight," he says slowly, and Chloe's face splits into a wide grin that makes it all worth it. "We'd have to leave soon, though," he says. "I wouldn't have time to take the bus with you to Sasha's."

"That's OK," I say quickly. "I can have Marianna

pick me up here. I'll tell her Chloe was helping me with my Carter application."

"Thanks, Ari," Chloe says. "You're a trouper." She brushes by me to get her purse and her phone.

"I can't believe I didn't remember earlier," I say, "but she asked me a couple of days ago and I sort of lost track of what night this is."

Gage is looking at me like he doesn't know whether to believe me or not.

"Call Marianna and make sure she can pick you up," he says.

I hold out my hand for his phone.

"Use the landline," says Chloe, pointing to the telephone on the kitchen counter. "You'll save minutes."

I pick up the phone and dial. "What's the address here?" I ask at some point in the phone call.

The call that I made to convince Gage.

The call that I faked.

'Cause I was just talking to the local weather recording.

32

TISSUES

As Chloe and Gage head down the stairs, I hear a guy say, "Hey, where's the little one?"

Gage says something I won't repeat, and one of the guys says, "Hey, easy, man. We're just having a little fun."

Then I hear Chloe say, "Forget them, Gage. We don't have time for this," and they're gone.

The silence in the apartment takes me by surprise. Even though I'd expected them to leave, I still can't quite believe that my plan worked. Gage will be mad when he gets home and finds that I'm still here — that I lied to him about staying at Sasha's and faked the call to Marianna — but I know he and

Chloe need a night out together. I know he'll eventually forgive me.

Although I can hear voices from downstairs, I feel a million miles away from anyone. The rooms are cavernous. I can see why Chloe wants more furniture, to make it feel more homey. My mind goes to where it usually does when we stay at Chloe's — to spreading out all my Paper Things. But I can't do that tonight. I can't bear to pull them out and see them ruined.

Then I remember that I haven't had dinner. I look in the freezer to see if there are any Hot Pockets. Nope. Only ice and something wrapped in foil — hamburger, maybe. The fridge has a Tupperware container of leftovers, but when I open it, I see white mold growing on the top.

The cabinet has more stuff than the refrigerator. I push around some flour, baking soda, bread crumbs, and a can of tomato paste, and behind them all is a half bag of potato chips, which I eat even though they are *incredibly* stale.

There is yelling in the stairwell.

Sirens wail.

A cockroach scurries along the kitchen floor and under the sink.

I try to turn on the TV, but the remote has so many buttons, it's hard to figure out. I push the button labeled "Power," but nothing happens. *What the . . . ?* I push and push and push, thinking it must take just the right touch, but nothing. Then I start pushing all of the buttons on the remote, one after another. All kinds of commands come up on the screen, but no TV. That's when I see another remote. I pick it up, press Power, and the screen is lit. I change the channel to HGTV, and there, thankfully, is my favorite show.

I get my blanket and pillow from behind the couch and stretch out. Almost immediately, I start to feel a little cheerier. I feel like I'm there with the young couple who are house hunting. Alongside them I walk into three different houses and ask, *Could this be my home?*

At the end of the show, the couple have a little party to celebrate their new home. There's a pitcher of lemonade on the table, and there are lots of platters with veggies and dips and cheese and crackers. Friends and family come to their house and tell them how beautiful it is. The woman points out her favorite corner, where she has a big, puffy chair with pillows. Behind her chair are shelves of books.

And then, suddenly, I start to cry. And not quiet little sniffling, but huge, full-body crying. I don't care how much noise I make in this echoey apartment that isn't mine. I don't care how much snot runs down my face. I just let myself sob.

But I'm not crying because the show reminded me that I don't have a home.

I am crying because I do have one.

I *do* have one.

And I miss it.

There is a sudden screeching, and it's loud—so loud that I know it's coming from inside the apartment. I blow my nose with a paper towel and search for the source of the noise. It doesn't take long to figure out that it's coming from the smoke detector in Nate and Cody's room. But I can't see any smoke and I can't smell a fire. I go over to their open window and look down. There are lots of people standing on the fire escape, smoking. Perhaps the smoke has drifted up here. Someone on the fire escape sees me and waves. I close the window all the way. But even with the window closed, the smoke detector doesn't stop screeching. It yells, and yells, and yells . . .

I grab a magazine from Nate's dresser, stand on the bed underneath the smoke detector, and fan the magazine frantically back and forth, back and forth, till it feels like my arm's going to fall off.

Eventually the wailing stops. I put the magazine back where I found it and wander into the kitchen.

Before I really even know what I'm doing, I pick up the phone and dial Janna's number.

She answers on the third ring. I tell her where I am and ask if she'll come get me. That's all. No small chat, no explanation. Just a question.

She's silent for a moment, and I hold my breath. "I'll be right there," she says.

I hang up and go sit on the couch to wait. Gage will be so mad when he finds out. . . . And hurt. But I can't help it.

I've made up my mind.

Just like that.

I'm going home.

· 33 ·
CONTRACTS

When Janna picks me up and I grab my backpack, she says, "Is that all you need?"

I nod but think, *No*. No, I need so much more than what is in my backpack. I need a homemade dinner, a warm shower, shampoo that smells like strawberries, a cozy bed. I need a place to keep my things, a place to do homework. I need a routine, a regular bedtime, a place to invite friends to. I need rules, all 465 of them.

I need the Queen of Rules.

"Where did you eat? Where did you sleep?" Janna asks, now that I've had a shower and am sitting at the kitchen table. "Did that apartment in the West End, the one where I dropped your things, did it ever belong to you?"

I don't want to provide details — details that will make it sound even worse than it was, details that will incriminate Gage. I simply shake my head no.

"I should have realized. I should have checked in with you more often. I should have talked with Human Services. I shouldn't have let my anger and resentment get so out of hand."

And your hurt feelings, I think but don't say. 'Cause I realize that a lot of what gets between Janna and Gage is their pride *and* their hurt feelings.

"It's funny," she says as she sets a grilled cheese-and-tomato sandwich in front of me. "Before I had you guys, I had all kinds of ideas about how kids should be brought up. When I first met you, I couldn't believe how lax your mother was. She seemed to ask so little of you and Gage, and you seemed to get away with so much. She never —"

"Gage is a good guy," I interrupt. "Responsible. We may not have had an apartment, but he took good care of me."

Janna nods. "You're right. In some ways, he's quite mature for a boy his age. I don't know why I couldn't see it before. I was so sure that he was going to turn out to be just like your father— impulsive and headstrong, following his passions and ignoring reality. But I've done a lot of soul-searching while you guys were away, and I think I might have misjudged your brother. Maybe your father, too."

I was tempted to tell Janna that I knew about her and our dad; maybe she'd feel she could open up to me then and explain what actually happened all those years ago, why she'd ripped all those pictures in half. But I worried that the only thing she'd hear was that I'd snooped in her scrapbooks, so I remained quiet, finishing my sandwich and wondering when Gage was going to call.

Wondering *if* he was going to call.

Before leaving Chloe's apartment, Janna had called Gage's phone and left him a message telling him that I was at her house. "Your sister has made a very difficult decision," she'd said, "and I know that she is worried about disappointing you. It would mean a great deal to her if you would stop by and talk to her. It would mean a great deal to me, too."

But that was two whole days ago, and he hasn't come by to see me. He hasn't even called. I'm starting to worry that I'll never see my brother again.

But finally, on the third day, he shows up.

Janna answers the door. I am lying on the couch watching House Hunters, which Janna has let me do a lot these past three days—probably because she can see that it's the only thing that makes me happy now that Gage has given up on me. I prop myself on my elbows when I hear his voice at the front door, but I stay hidden behind some pillows, listening in.

"Thank you for coming," I hear Janna say.

Gage mutters something in reply, but I can't make it out. Then: "Is Ari here?"

"She is," Janna says. "Would you like me to go get her?"

Again, Gage mutters something that's too low for me to hear. But Janna doesn't come for me, and I hear chairs scraping across the kitchen floor, so I guess he didn't say, "Yes, please go get my sister. I miss her terribly!"

"Like I said, this was a very difficult decision for her," Janna says calmly. "She didn't want to hurt you."

"I hate knowing that she lied about staying at Sasha's because she was trying to take care of *me*," says Gage. "It was my job to look after *her*."

I want to rush over and interrupt him, but I don't know what to say.

"It's not easy looking after a kid," says Janna. "You make some decent calls, and some that, well . . . let's just say that making mistakes is a whole lot easier than you think it will be."

"Yeah, I'd like a couple of do-overs," says Gage, and then there's some mumbling that I can't hear. I picture Janna and Gage nodding in agreement, maybe for the first time ever.

"So, what now?" Gage asks.

"Your room is still available," Janna says, which I know is her way of asking him to move back in.

I hold my breath. I want to say *please, please, please,* but I don't.

"I think it'd be best for everyone if I lived on my own. My friend West thinks he might be able to set me up with this stability program, which will help get me on my feet. I'll be able to take classes, maybe even start at Port City Community College."

"I'd like to help you in any way I can," says Janna. "I know that we've butted heads in the past, but I really do want what's best for you—and for Ari. You'll let me know if you need help?" she asks, and her voice is more vulnerable than I've ever heard it.

Gage mumbles his thanks. I don't really believe that he would reach out to Janna for help, but at least he isn't throwing that in her face like in the old days.

"I should talk to Ari now," he finally says.

"It's about time!" I say, popping up from the couch.

Gage smiles when he sees me, and I can tell that no matter how sad my decision has made him, no matter how disappointed he is in me, he still loves me.

I'm not prepared for the tears that come when he

hugs me, though. "What's all this?" Gage asks, pulling back to look at me with concern.

"I'll give you two some privacy," says Janna, and she heads upstairs.

"I'm sorry!" I say, sniffling. "I'm sorry I left you. I'm sorry I broke our promise to Mama. I'm sorry I let you down."

"Ari, Ari," he soothes, steering me into a chair at the table next to his. "You didn't let me down. I let *you* down. I never should have taken you from here without an apartment lined up. And I shouldn't have left you alone at Chloe's just so we could go to a stupid concert."

"You didn't leave me," I say. "I tricked you. You thought I was going to Sasha's."

"Still," he says, and then is quiet.

"I need you to know something," I say. I take a breath. "I didn't call Janna because I didn't want to be with you anymore. I loved being with you. But— I know this sounds stupid—but here at Janna's . . . here I get to be a kid. Just a kid."

Gage looks into his folded hands as if they

hold some sort of answer and then finally nods his head. "You know, you're pretty smart for a kid."

Gage and I catch up for a while—he tells me about the concert and Chloe and his job at Jiffy Lube, and I tell him my plans for my presentation— and then Janna reappears, looking tentative.

Gage beckons her into the kitchen with a nod.

"I thought it might be helpful if we were to work out some sort of schedule," she says. "So you guys can do things together regularly."

I look at Gage, wondering if he'll be upset at Janna for wanting to make everything so organized. But his expression remains calm.

"And when I finally get an apartment," says Gage, "maybe we can talk about this again?"

"Of course," says Janna.

But I think we all know that I won't be moving in with Gage. "We don't have to be in the same house to be family," I say. "Whether we live together or not, we stick together—right?"

"Right," says Gage.

"That's what your mama wanted," Janna says.

And I know she's right.

Gage gets up to go. I give him the biggest hug I can, and he's still got an arm around me when he turns to Janna and says, "There's something I've always wanted to know."

Janna, who's busy picking lint off the arm of her sweater, looks up at him.

I stop breathing. His voice is suddenly tense, and I'm afraid he's going to start another fight, raising tensions all over again.

"Why didn't you ever adopt us?"

Janna opens her mouth to reply, but no words escape. She closes it again and seems to try out different answers in her mind until she finds just the right one. When she answers, it's almost a whisper. "I was afraid that if I asked to adopt you, you'd say no."

That's not the answer Gage expected, I can tell. He doesn't say anything right away, like he, too, is thinking carefully. "No one can replace our mom," he says, but the words aren't angry and defensive, like they used to be. Instead, they are gentle, reassuring. "But if we'd known . . . if we'd known that's what you wanted, well, then, maybe that could have been OK."

Janna's whole expression softens, as if she's just realized something huge. "You thought I didn't want you. You thought I'd taken you and Ari in because I felt obligated to. Oh, Gage."

She gets up and takes a step toward him. He flinches, but she doesn't let that stop her.

And then I see something I never thought I'd see.

I see Janna hugging Gage. And I see Gage letting her.

HATS

The rumor in the hallways at school is that Crazy Hat Day is going to be this coming Friday, three days from today. Kids whisper the news between classes and clam up whenever a teacher walks by. Daniel asks me why I'm letting Keisha organize Crazy Hat Day when it was my idea in the first place. I tell him that she'll be able to make it a much bigger success than I ever could.

Besides, I have another idea for how to contribute to one of my favorite Eastland Elementary traditions.

When Gage came over to Janna's, he brought all of the clothes that I had left at Chloe's and Briggs's.

He also brought my piggy bank. "Now you can buy something for yourself," he said.

After school, Janna takes me to the bank, where the coin machine tallies up my savings: $47.23. ("All from collecting coins on the street?" Janna asks incredulously. I smile and tell her that all kinds of valuable things are around us — we just have to open our eyes.)

Next we head to the One Stop Party Shop, where I buy cheap paper chef hats, pipe cleaners, sports decals, flowers, stick-on bull horns, ribbons, googly eyes, and weird little rubber-alien toys. Briggs is working, and he doesn't seem surprised to see me with Janna, which I guess means that Gage told him that I'd moved back home. He tells me he's missed having me around, which I think he's saying just to be nice, and then he offers to let me use his employee discount. Thanks to Briggs, I end up having a little money left over, which I put right back in my piggy bank.

On Thursday, I wait till the end of social studies to approach Mr. O.

"I'm very impressed with your report on Louisa May Alcott," Mr. O. says, and I feel myself blushing with pride. It's been a long time since a teacher complimented me on my schoolwork, and I hadn't realized just how much I missed being a shining star. "Are you all set for your presentation next week?" he asks.

I nod, thinking of the computer classes with Ms. Finch, and how I'm hoping to incorporate some of what I've learned there into my presentation next Tuesday.

"Mr. O.," I begin, hoping I'm not about to ruin the mood. "Remember last week when we talked about civil disobedience?"

Mr. O. cocks an eyebrow. "Yes. . . . What exactly do you have in mind, Arianna?"

I hitch my backpack higher up on my shoulders. "Keisha is organizing a Crazy Hat Day tomorrow," I confide, hoping that I haven't misjudged Mr. O. and that he'll keep it a secret from Mr. Chandler. "And I thought it would be nice if as many people as possible could make hats—not just the kids she thinks to tell about it."

Mr. O. is nodding along but has yet to say anything.

"So I was wondering if I could set up a crafts table outside your room. I bought all the supplies," I add in a rush so that he doesn't think I'm asking him to help with that. "But I thought it would be good to have a place where kids can make their own hats if they want to. That way, no one will feel left out."

"I don't think in front of my classroom is an appropriate place for such a table," Mr. O. says, his expression serious.

My stomach drops. Just like that, I've gone from being a shining star to being Arianna Hazard, problem student.

"I think that such a table really ought to be set up somewhere more central," he continues. "Like in the front hall."

I blink. "Near Mr. Chandler's office?"

"Those who engage in acts of civil disobedience must be very brave," he says.

"Holy moly!" I whisper. But I know in my heart that he's right: if Crazy Hat Day is going to be a success, it needs to be front and center, where no one can miss it — especially Mr. Chandler.

"Thanks, Mr. O.! I mean, Mr. O'Neil!" I say, practically skipping out of his room.

"Just stay away from the glitter!" Mr. O. calls after me.

I'm excited to tell Daniel about my hat-making-table idea, but when I find him during lunch, he looks unconvinced.

"I don't know . . ." he says, picking at his hot lunch. "Won't people think it's kind of lame?"

I scoff. "Since when do you care if people think something's lame?" I ask. I actually mean it as a compliment; Daniel is one of the bravest kids I know, always willing to march to his own drumbeat even if it means being laughed at or being sent to the principal's office. But I can tell by the look on his face that he doesn't take it that way.

"I don't really care if people like Keisha and Sasha think it's lame," I say. "I want to have a station for kids who want to make a crazy hat but maybe can't afford to, or who weren't told about Crazy Hat Day because Keisha didn't think they were cool enough to be looped in. The whole point of Crazy Hat Day is that *everybody* gets to do it, not just the cool, popular kids."

Daniel looks at me like he's trying to figure me out. Maybe it's because up until recently, I was basically one of those cool, popular kids—never quite as popular as Keisha and her crew, but not exactly someone who worried about what the poor kids or the unpopular kids were going through.

And suddenly I decide that I want someone—I want *Daniel*—to know what's changed.

I take a deep breath and tell him that for the past six weeks, Gage and I were on our own, hopping from place to place, sometimes staying at shelters, sometimes eating at the soup kitchen. At first I hear my voice waver 'cause I'm embarrassed to be admitting all of this, but the more I talk and the more Daniel listens without judging, the more I realize that I don't have to be ashamed of my truth. That Gage and I were still the same people we'd always been, even if the circumstances we were living in looked pretty different.

"We were actually really lucky," I say, realizing, perhaps for the first time, just how true this is. "We had friends who helped us along the way. We were never truly on our own."

"Wow," he says quietly.

I'm quiet for a moment, too, stuck in some of those memories. My thoughts flash briefly to my Paper Things. But even that ache has dulled, like the wound is already starting to heal.

"Anyway," I say, "that's why I want to make it easy for kids to make hats. And I was kind of hoping that you'd work the hat table with me."

Daniel looks serious, and I'm afraid he's going to say no. Is it because he's embarrassed to be seen with me in such a public place?

"It depends," he says at last. "Will you jump off the bleachers with me?"

"No way!" I say. "I already told you—"

Daniel holds up a finger to stop me. Then he pulls out my note, which is nearly worn to tatters, and reads aloud:

*"I have thought of two activities for numbers
seven and eight, and if you'll do those, I'll do two
of your items with you. OK?*

    *7. Help Arianna Hazard get a leadership
       role.*

    8. Help Arianna Hazard apply to Carter."

"But we didn't do either of those things," I point
out. "I never got a leadership role and we never filled
out my application to Carter."

"Yeah, but you're on your way, right?"

This time I don't argue with Daniel. I may not
have an Eastland leadership role or a completed
application to Carter, but I've found my own way to
be a leader, and for the first time, I understand why
Daniel is less concerned than the rest of us about
where he goes to school next year. You can be your
best self no matter where you are.

"So you'll do it?" he asks.

"I'll think about it," I say.

· 35 ·
NEWSPAPERS

My stomach is *très* rolly as I walk to school on Friday morning. I'm worried that Mr. Chandler is going to be furious. I'm worried that Daniel won't join me at the table in front of the whole school. But most of all, I'm worried that I'm going to throw up again.

"Hello, there, Ari!" a voice calls to me as I near the bus stop. I look around and spot Reggie — and Amelia — across the street.

"Reggie!" I shout, waving happily. "Hi!" I wait till the road is clear and then dash across to Reggie's side of the street.

"How have you guys been?" I ask, scratching

Amelia behind the ears. Her tail swings wildly.

"Can't complain," Reggie says, which is something I like about him. He's always looking on the bright side of things.

"The weather's warming up," I say, raising my face a bit to greet the morning sun. "That makes everything better."

"Indeed, it does," he agrees. "And it makes for good paper wishplane flying."

I look at him curiously.

"You haven't heard?" he asks. "I'm working at the different shelters here in Port City. I happened to tell someone who works at the men's shelter about your plane, and the one I made for your friend—you know, the one who wanted the bike?"

I nod, encouraging him to go on.

"Well, as it turns out, there's this program to help folks set goals and then take baby steps toward making them happen. I sit down with individuals— or sometimes families—and listen to their hopes. Then I help them fold a wishplane—one chosen especially for them. I guess the people who hired me think that it's helpful for people to zoom in on a goal—"

"And launch it into the air!" I finish for him.

Reggie laughs. "Yup, literally!"

"That's so cool!" I say, hoping this means that there's more money for dog food for Amelia—and maybe even a little left over for Reggie.

"Say, that's some hat you've got there," Reggie says, just now noticing the hat I'm carrying.

"Oh, this," I say, laughing. "It's a crazy tradition at my school, but one that's super fun. My mom actually made a hat just like this one when she was my age," I say proudly.

"Can I see it on you?" Reggie asks, his eyes kind.

"Sure!" I say, and I model the hat for him.

"It's beautiful," he says. And I know that he means it.

Suddenly all that nervousness from earlier just kind of melts away. My hat *is* beautiful, and it's a direct connection to Mama and to the whole history of Eastland Elementary School. Whatever happens today, however much trouble I get into, I know it will all have been worth it.

"I better go. But it was good seeing you, Reggie. You, too, Amelia!"

"Bye, Ari," Reggie says. "Thanks for everything."

Hearing Reggie thank me has the same effect as hearing Mr. O. tell me that he was impressed with my paper on Louisa May Alcott. However silly I might look on the outside, inside I am positively glowing.

I might not be nervous about Crazy Hat Day anymore, but I can tell that lots of other kids are. I see a group of kids getting off the bus with their hats in their hands—unlike on past Crazy Hat Days, when everyone would proudly sport their silly hats from the moment they left their houses till the bus dropped them off back at home.

Keisha is standing front and center by the double doors. She's wearing a bright-red crab hat with boingy eyes waving on top, and she's encouraging everyone to put their hats on, too. "C'mon, guys! Show your school spirit! Show Principal Chandler that we value our Eastland Tigers traditions!"

I have to say, Keisha's enthusiasm is catching. I

watch as a bunch of kids put on their hats, looking braver after hearing Keisha's motivating words. No wonder she got assigned three leadership roles—and no wonder Sasha wants to be her friend. Keisha actually seems pretty cool.

Before you know it, more kids have hats on than don't. Even the first- and second-graders!

I find Daniel lingering in the main hall.

"Ready?" he asks.

"Ready as I'll ever be," I say, but I'm smiling. Together we set up the crafts table and start calling out to the kids who don't have hats.

"Hats here! Come make your crazy hats!"

"We've got stickers! We've got pipe cleaners! We've got toys! Whatever your hat needs, we've got you covered!"

A third-grade girl wanders over. "My mom wouldn't let me wear a hat to school," she says.

"Well, you can make one here if you want."

She spots the fake flowers and brightens, though she still hesitates.

Other kids wander over to see what we've got, but none will start creating. None, that is, until Matthew

Stone, one of the soccer stars, comes over. He's wearing a camouflage hat, but it's not exactly crazy. So he starts gluing aliens to it. "Check this out!" he shouts to a group of his friends. His friends wander over and start gluing things to their hats, too. Then more kids come over and start decorating their hats or making new ones, each one crazier than the last.

I'm helping the third-grade girl attach some pipe cleaners to her hat when I look over her shoulder and see Mr. Chandler coming. He's walking down the hall, and there's no question: he's headed straight to our table.

PERMISSION SLIPS

"Mr. Chandler! Mr. Chandler!"

Before Mr. Chandler reaches our table, his secretary comes up behind him and waylays him.

"You'd better get outside," she says, panting slightly. "There's a reporter from the *Port City Times* talking with Keisha Cooper. And she's got a photographer with her, too."

I crane my neck, trying to see out the row of windows behind me, but all I can see are trees and students milling around.

"Why don't you go check it out," Daniel says to me. "I'll watch the table."

The morning bell rings, but word has spread

about the reporter, and rather than heading to their classes, kids pour outside, eager to mug for the camera.

I push my way through the throng until I can see Keisha, who's standing very straight and speaking to a reporter while she takes notes.

"This is an act of civil disobedience," Keisha says. "As you know, Henry David Thoreau and Rosa Parks both acted on their ideals and helped raise awareness of the need for change. We're all wearing crazy hats today to bring back Eastland Elementary's traditions, to let Principal Chandler know that even though the traditions might not appear on academic tests, they're still important. They give us common experiences and help us feel like we're part of a community."

"Now, listen here," a voice says, directly behind me. It's Mr. Chandler! He directs a few students to get out of his way and suddenly he's standing next to me.

The reporter quickly thanks Keisha and then turns to Mr. Chandler. "Mr. Chandler, what do you make of this student protest?"

The photographer snaps a few photos of Mr. Chandler. I step back, hoping I'm not in the shots.

"As I've explained to students and faculty alike, these so-called traditions are frivolous and disrupt learning. Just take a look around! Valuable learning is being disrupted at this very moment. Students are not in class, where they are supposed to be; instead, they're making hats in the hallways and trying to get their picture in the newspaper!"

"Isn't it possible," says the reporter, "that important lessons are being learned by this protest?"

"'Protest' is a rather grand word for this . . . display," Mr. Chandler says. "But why don't you come and talk inside, so that our students can get to their required classes." Then he turns and directs all of us back to our classrooms.

I slip away from the crowd and rush back to the table to tell Daniel what happened. I'm in the middle of my story when his eyes go big and he points behind me.

I cringe and turn around slowly, expecting to see a glowering Mr. Chandler.

Instead, I see the news reporter and photographer.

"What's going on here?" the reporter asks.

She looks nice, but all I can focus on is her pencil poised in the air, ready to take down my every awkward word.

"This is a station for kids to make a crazy hat if they don't have one," Daniel says, leaning forward on the table.

The reporter scribbles in her notebook, and the photographer clicks away. "Has this table always been a part of the Hat Day tradition here at Eastland?" the reporter asks.

"No," says Daniel. "Ari came up with the idea. She's actually the one who started this whole campaign. A few weeks ago, she organized a secret spring blizzard, where we decorated the hallway with paper snowflakes just like we used to do for the first snowfall. Right, Ari?" he says.

The reporter swivels back toward me, but I'm still frozen.

"Ari, tell them why you wanted to reestablish the traditions," Daniel urges.

I think back to our spring blizzard and how Daniel had wanted me to tell Mr. Chandler why the

Eastland traditions mattered so much—not just to me personally but to all of us. I threw up before I got the chance to explain things to him. But right here, right now, with the reporter looking at me, I realize that this might be my one chance to tell my story.

And before I can change my mind, I start talking.

"I know what it's like to be an outsider, to feel like you don't belong. For six weeks, my brother and I were, well, homeless. We slept on couches and at the shelter and even in a car. We did the best we could, but my grades still suffered, and I even lost my best friend because of it. Because I was too embarrassed to tell anyone what was really going on. Because I didn't want to be different. One of the best things about the Eastland Elementary traditions is that they let everyone feel like part of the same community, just like Keisha said. And I wanted to make sure that everyone who wanted to be a part of Crazy Hat Day had that opportunity—whatever their lives are like or whatever group they belong to. We're all Eastland Tigers, and this is our way of saying that."

The reporter smiles and nods at the photographer, apparently signaling that our interview is over. She asks Daniel and me for our names — she even makes us spell them — and then they hurry off toward Mr. Chandler's office.

I turn to Daniel, my cheeks suddenly burning. "Did I really just tell that reporter that I was homeless for six weeks?"

Daniel smiles. "You did! It was awesome! I wish I was half as brave as you are, Arianna Hazard!"

I laugh. "I guess I am brave!"

"Yeah," he says, "but brave enough to jump from the bleachers?"

I spend the rest of the day waiting for Mr. Chandler's voice to come over the loudspeaker to call me and Daniel down to his office. I also keep expecting him to demand that students remove their hats — or the teachers to demand it — but no one does, even though the reporter is long gone.

Then, during social studies, the intercom hums to life, and Mr. Chandler's gruff voice crackles into Mr. O.'s classroom: "Attention, students. After discussing the matter with the members of the Port City School Board, I have decided to reinstate the

Eastland Elementary traditions. Those of you wearing hats today may continue to do so. In addition, we will be holding the fifth-grade library sleepover sometime in May. Permission slips will be going home with all eligible fifth-graders at the beginning of next week."

A roar of cheers and applause can be heard from all the classrooms in the fifth-grade wing—and probably everywhere else in the school, too. We did it! We really did it!

Amid the excitement, though, something gives me pause. What exactly did Mr. Chandler mean when he said "all *eligible* fifth-graders"?

· 37 ·
HEARTS

As I leave school, Sasha is standing outside the doors. Her time as patrol leader is up and she is back to being one of the walkers. I can't help but hope that she's waiting for me.

She is.

As surprised as I am that she's waiting for me, I'm even more surprised that she's alone, with no Linnie or Keisha in sight.

"Hey," I say, feeling oddly shy around my former best friend.

"Hey," she says, falling into step next to me. We walk together in silence for a ways. I feel like she wants to say something to me, but I can't for the life of me figure out what it could be.

"So . . . Fiona overheard you talking to that reporter this morning," Sasha says.

My stomach drops. I didn't remember there being anyone else except Daniel in the hallway when I was being interviewed—but then again, I hadn't really been able to see anything but the camera.

"And . . . ?" I ask finally, unable to stand the silence.

"*And,*" Sasha says, as we meander toward Head Start together, "she says you told the reporter that you were *homeless.*"

My skin prickles with shame, but I hold my chin up and look Sasha in the eyes. "I did. Because I was."

Sasha stops and stares at me, challenging me with her eyes.

"What happened? Did Janna lose her condo? And why didn't you tell me?"

"Gage and I moved out of Janna's place for a while. They needed a break from each other, and I went with Gage. But it was harder being on our own than we'd realized it would be."

Sasha puts her hands on her hips. "You still haven't said why you didn't tell me. Did you think I'd be mean about it? That I wouldn't understand?"

"I'm not sure," I say, shrugging. "Maybe." I think about reminding her of the time she and Linnie and Keisha whisper-talked about how greasy my hair looked and how I smelled, but I decide not to. "But mostly I didn't want you to feel bad for me—again. I'm so tired of being *poor Ari.*"

We continue walking without saying anything. "You know, I get how you were feeling," Sasha says at last. "I got sick and tired of being *Ari's shadow.*"

"My shadow?"

"You've always been the better student, the teachers' favorite. So, when your grades started slipping and I got the leadership role but you didn't, I thought maybe it was my turn to be the one in the spotlight."

"And you thought I was ignoring you? That I was angry because you'd started to get some recognition?"

"Something like that."

"I wouldn't do that, Sasha," I say. "That's no way to treat a best friend."

I wonder if Sasha is going to correct me, to tell me that she's my *former* best friend, but instead she says, "If we all get into Carter, do you think you could learn to be friends with Keisha, too?"

I think about how cool Keisha was this morning, getting kids to wear their hats and speaking eloquently to the news reporter. "Sure," I say. "But I doubt I'll get in to Carter. I haven't even sent in my application yet—and I've just announced to a reporter that I was homeless for six weeks!"

Sasha screws up her face at that. "They can't deny you a spot because you were homeless. That's, like, unconstitutional or something. And applications aren't due till tomorrow. There's still time."

We part ways at the Laundromat, just like always. As I watch Sasha head home, I realize that she's right. It's not too late—not for Carter, and maybe not for us.

• • •

At Head Start I show the kids my crazy hat, and of course they want to make hats, too. Since Fran and Carol weren't prepared to make hats today, Fran persuades the kids to make crowns instead. She helps them cut a jagged strip from construction paper that the kids can decorate with pom-poms and glitter. Then she staples the crowns to fit their heads. By the end of the afternoon, all the children have crowns, and their cheeks and noses are sparkling with glitter.

I'm just about to leave for the day, when Carol asks if perhaps I'd like to come to Head Start in the mornings during the summer. I hadn't thought of working past graduation, but it occurs to me that Janna might want to keep on working as a nurse, and coming to Head Start would give me something to do while she's at work. I tell her I'll check with Janna.

Gage picks me up today, just like old times. Janna's working this evening; Gage and I are going to Flatbread for pizza. As soon as we've walked out the door, he tells me that he's going to have a room all his own at the stability house that West told him about, and that the people who run it have already helped him set up a savings account.

While listening to Gage's ideas for the future, I hear Fran call good-bye. I turn to wave, and I see her—not behind us, not walking to the bus stop as usual, but pedaling away on a bike. I can't wait to hear how that happened!

That night, I work on the application for Carter Middle School. Fortunately the blanks for address and name of guardian are now easy to fill in. For one of the questions, I write about my experience working with the kids at Head Start and about coming up with the idea for Reggie's paper wishplanes. I don't know if these are the sorts of things that will impress the Carter people, but they're my truth.

I stare at the last question, the one that basically asks you to describe what sets you apart from your peers, what makes you special—what makes you Carter material.

I wonder if the people at Carter will read about me in the newspaper, talking about my experiences being homeless. That sure sets me apart. Maybe Sasha's right, and they can't legally discriminate against me for something like that, but I still can't really believe that a school like Carter would want to admit a student whose most noteworthy quality is that she didn't have a home for a month and a half.

I push the application aside. Maybe in the morning I'll have the answer to the final essay question. But I sure don't have it now.

· 38 ·
SCRAPS

I come downstairs to breakfast, and Janna, coffee cup in hand, is hunched over something at the breakfast bar. Her facial expression goes from smiling to a moment of sadness and then back to pleasure again.

"What are you reading?" I ask. She gets up from her seat, motioning for me to sit down, to see for myself. It's the morning newspaper, and on the front page is a picture of me in my crazy hat, and the headline:

HOMELESS GIRL PROVIDES MEANS FOR OTHER
STUDENTS TO UPHOLD VALUED TRADITIONS

My stomach drops. I lean back in the chair, waiting for her to yell at me for airing my private business in front of the whole world, for being disloyal to her and to Gage.

Instead, though, she clears her throat and reads the article aloud:

"Ask anyone who attended Eastland Elementary School in the past twenty years and they will happily tell you about the school's April First tradition: Crazy Hat Day. This year, however, Mr. Chandler, the newly appointed principal at the elementary school, abolished the practice, along with many of the school's other traditions, citing a need to focus on academic standards instead.

"Today, in a protest led by Keisha Cooper, students wore crazy hats to express the importance of these traditions and the role they play in building a learning community. This isn't the first time students have indicated their dissatisfaction with the changes at Eastland. Earlier this month, Arianna Hazard (who is credited with having had the original idea of a civic protest) and Daniel Huber hung snowflakes throughout the halls to bring attention to the issue.

"At the onset of Crazy Hat Day, Ms. Hazard was found at a crafts table she set up to provide materials for students to make their own hats if needed. Many weeks of homelessness have made Arianna Hazard particularly sensitive to students who might be in need of extra support.

"'One of the best things about the Eastland Elementary traditions is that they let everyone feel like part of the same community, just like Keisha said,' explained Ms. Hazard. 'And I wanted to make sure that everyone who wanted to be a part of Crazy Hat Day had that opportunity—whatever their lives are like or whatever group they belong to. We're all Eastland Tigers, and this is our way of saying that.'

"Thanks to the efforts of students like Arianna Hazard, Daniel Huber, and Keisha Cooper, the voices of the students were heard. By the end of the day, the Port City School Board agreed to reinstate these long-standing traditions."

Janna puts the paper down.

"I'm so sorry," I say in a rush. "I know I shouldn't have said anything, and maybe now you'll get in trouble or Gage will, and I've blown my chance at getting into Carter, which is all Mama ever wanted for me, but—"

"Hush, Ari," Janna interrupts. Then she leaves the room.

I stand in the kitchen, fighting back tears. What have I done?

Just then, Janna returns, carrying a scrapbook. One with my name on it! She takes the scissors from the utility drawer, picks up the newspaper, and cuts out the article.

She opens the scrapbook. As she flips through the pages, I catch glimpses of pictures—pictures of me, and of Gage, and of me and Gage. Pictures of Mama and of the three of us together. Pictures that I thought were lost for good. All this time, Janna had kept them safe in a scrapbook.

About halfway through the scrapbook, the pictures stop being familiar. And I realize that somehow, without our ever realizing it, Janna had been taking pictures of me and Gage, documenting our time here with her. There're pictures of us leaving for school, pictures of us cleaning up after dinner, pictures of us laughing together in the living room. Just everyday moments caught on camera—and saved in a book.

Janna stops at a blank page near the back, takes a glue stick from her pocket, applies glue to the back of the article, and carefully pastes it in the book. Above it, with a black Sharpie, she writes: *Proud Moment*.

"I know that you and Gage hold your mother's wishes for you close to your hearts, and I support that," Janna says slowly. "But you've got to understand that she would never want *any* of her wishes to cause suffering. Your mother wanted you and Gage to love and support each other always—no matter where each of you was living—and that's what you'll do.

"And your mother wanted you to go to Carter because she wanted you to shine. But, Arianna Hazard, you can shine wherever you are. That doesn't come from the school. That comes from you."

She points to the picture of me in my crazy hat. "See! Look at you, girl!"

Tears fill my eyes, and I blink them away. I stare at those words emblazoned above the article: *Proud Moment*. Janna isn't ashamed of me, or of Gage.

She's proud of us. She's always been proud of us. And she knew my mama better than anyone.

"Could you take me to Office Mart later?" I ask suddenly.

"What for?"

"I'd like to make a copy of the article for my Carter application."

In the end, the people at Carter might not choose me, but at least they will have gotten to know me — the me that my experiences have helped me to become.

39

REPORT CARDS

Coming back to school on Monday isn't easy. Janna had reacted well to my public announcement that I'd been homeless, but I have no idea how kids at school will act. Fortunately, Sasha and Keisha are right there, waiting for me at my locker.

"Did you see the front page of the paper, Ari?" Keisha asks. "Wasn't that cool?"

I am relieved to hear Keisha's enthusiasm—and to know that she didn't mind sharing the spotlight—but I also can't help noticing that Sasha's quiet words of agreement are just that—quiet. I hope she isn't feeling as if she's being pushed into the shadows again.

Throughout the day kids approach me to ask questions or make comments about my homelessness. Some are awkward: "Did you have to ask people for money?" or "Was it scary being on the streets?" Some are very personal: "Why would you leave the home you had?" At first, these questions make me nervous, and I'm afraid to answer. Afraid that my answers will lead to teasing. But as the day wears on and I have more conversations, I realize that kids are just being curious, that everyone wonders whether something like homelessness could ever happen to them, and I try to answer as honestly as I can without getting defensive.

During final announcements, Mr. Chandler tells us that the fifth-grade sleepover will be on May 11 — two weeks before graduation and one week before applicants hear whether they've been accepted to Carter. "Eligible fifth-graders will have completed all their assignments, paid any library fines they may have, and have consistently exhibited good Eastland citizenship throughout the school year."

Good citizenship? As I ponder this last requirement, I notice that Mr. O. is looking right at me.

"Will we have a presentation tomorrow, as promised, Ms. Hazard?"

The kids laugh. At the end of the day, my last name is still the funniest thing about me.

Right after dinner, I ask Janna if she'll listen as I practice my presentation. I know she'll find areas for improvement. As I click on my slide presentation on her computer, I can tell that she's especially pleased with my subject—and touched that I chose someone who she introduced to me.

"Did you know that Louisa May Alcott was a nurse, like you?" I ask her.

She nods. "During the Civil War," she says. "And just like me, she raised a little girl whose mother had died."

I smile at these connections between Janna and Louisa May Alcott. But, as I'm clicking through slides about Louisa's *Little Women*, I recognize another connection that I hadn't made until now. Every reader of *Little Women* thinks that the main character, Jo, will marry her best friend, Laurie. But she doesn't. Laurie marries Jo's sister Amy instead.

I turn to Janna with my mouth wide open.

"What?" she asks, and suddenly I'm scrambling for a careful response. "What?" she repeats.

I give up and blurt, "Why did my father marry Mama instead of you?"

She gives me a look of total surprise, and I'm afraid that she's going to ask me how I know about her relationship with my father—that I'm going to have to confess to snooping—but she doesn't. Maybe she assumes that Gage told me, or maybe she's more concerned with my question than how I arrived at it.

She shakes her head as if trying to clear out what's not important. "Relationships can be very complicated," she says. "I think I was trying too hard to shape your father into the man I wanted him to be. I had a specific course for the two of us, and I was forever outlining my plans. Your mother was different; she was more playful, more spontaneous, and more accepting. I think your father liked who he was when he was around her."

"Was it terrible when he chose my mother instead of you?"

Janna's silent for a moment and then nods. "They broke my heart, and I'll tell you now, I was not forgiving. In fact, I was rather hateful. I never thought your mother would get back in touch with me."

I've always wondered why Mama chose Janna to raise us instead of someone who knew us better, like Marianna, and now I feel even *more* confused.

Janna must have been thinking along the same lines. "I guess your mother figured that since I had loved your father at one time and had cared deeply for her, I'd have no trouble loving you and Gage as well. And she was right, of course. Though I know now that I took out some of my old hurt on you guys, especially Gage."

It's in this moment that I realize that Janna is the only person I know who knew, really knew, both my parents. Suddenly I have a million questions: *Did my father like to read? What kind of music did he listen to? Was he shy?*

Maybe when my application to Carter is completed and my social studies presentation is finished, I'll ask Janna these questions. And maybe, just maybe, I'll start to get a sense of the dad I never knew.

40

SHEET MUSIC

My presentation on Tuesday goes very well. Instead of using animation or movie clips as I thought I might, I stop my slide show midway and present a little melodrama—a short old-fashioned play that has lots of scary action—just like the plays that Louisa May Alcott used to perform with her family, and like her characters performed in her books. I thought of asking Sasha and Keisha, and maybe even Daniel, to help me with the performance, but in the end, I decide to play all the parts myself. This time I'm *trying* to make my classmates laugh, and I succeed.

I knew that I wanted to end my presentation with one of Louisa May Alcott's quotes. At first I was going to use this one:

Far away there in the sunshine are my highest aspirations. I may not reach them, but I can look up and see their beauty, believe in them, and try to follow where they lead.

But finally I decide on this one:

My book came out; and people began to think that topsy-turvy Louisa would amount to something after all.

Which didn't remind me of Janna.

It reminded me of myself.

When my presentation is over, Mr. O. pulls me aside to tell me that not only have I done well, but I've also satisfied the requirements for attendance at the fifth-grade sleepover! Thankfully, my good citizenship (or lack of) was never mentioned by anyone.

On the night of the fifth-grade sleepover, droves of kids arrive at Eastland Elementary with sleeping bags in their arms. I've no sooner gotten out of Janna's car when Daniel grabs me.

"Are you going to help me free Gerald?" he asks.

"No way," I say. "He'd never survive."

"Jump from the bleachers?"

I don't get a chance to object, because at that moment, Sasha pulls me away. "Hurry," she says. The girls are sleeping in the library and we won't get a good spot unless we spread our sleeping bags out now."

"Meet me in the art room at nine," Daniel says.

Ugh, I think, suspecting what Daniel wants. The art room is close to the polished math hallway.

After claiming our place in the mystery section of the library, Keisha, Sasha, and I head to the cafeteria for dinner. The teachers, wearing their own crazy hats, are serving us pizza from boxes tonight. I laugh when I see Ms. Finch wearing a hat piled high with birds.

I'm at a table surrounded by girls I've known most of my life. We're recalling Eastland memories, laughing at all the silly things that happened over the years. Just as I start to remind everyone of how frightened we were in first grade when Smokey the Bear came to school, I hear someone singing. Others hear it, too, and we turn to see where the music is coming from.

It's Daniel. Of course, it's Daniel. He's standing on a bench, trying to lead the entire fifth grade in a chorus of "Eensy-Weensy Spider." A kindergarten song.

No one joins in.

I look to the teachers, hoping that they'll stop him. *End his humiliation,* I think. *He'll still get to check off number 5 on his bucket list.*

They don't stop him, and he moves on to sing "Five Little Monkeys Jumping on the Bed"—all five verses.

A few kids make the hand motions, but none will join in the singing.

Daniel looks at me as if to say, *Come on, Ari. I sat in the front hallway behind the crafts table for you. You owe me this.*

And I do owe him this moment—I know I do. But still I can't do it. I can't bring myself to sing.

Daniel finishes "Five Little Monkeys," and there's silence. I guess everyone is wondering what he'll do next.

If I've learned anything this year, it's that Daniel Huber is persistent. He starts to sing "Food Group Boogie," and a few kids laugh. A few quiet voices join in.

I look over at Sasha to see if she's rolling her eyes. She glances at me and then without saying a word, she jumps up and starts singing and dancing along with Daniel. Then she gives me the biggest, brightest smile, which says, *I bet you didn't expect this!*

I sure didn't. Not for a moment. But there's lots that I don't know about Sasha—and lots that she still doesn't know about me—and I make a quick wish that we'll have lots of time together at Carter to learn those things.

Her actions are contagious. "Food Group Boogie" is just wild enough, just bizarre enough, that everyone in the room eventually gets to their feet to join them. Even me.

We go from singing "Food Group Boogie" to "If You're Happy and You Know It," and then "The Hokey Pokey." Not one student sits out. I catch Hannah's eye across the cafeteria, and we exchange smiles.

Daniel reminds all of us that tonight, despite our plans for the future, we are all Eastland Tigers.

It's nine o'clock and I'm nervous. Was Daniel serious about meeting him in the art room? The entire fifth-grade class is gathered in the auditorium, watching a movie. If I slip out and get caught wandering the halls, I worry that I'll blow any last chance I have of getting accepted to Carter. Still, I feel like I already let Daniel down once tonight and I don't want to do it again.

I get up from my chair in the gym and move toward the back doors, hoping that any teacher watching me will just assume that I'm heading to the girls' room. The halls are dimly lit and totally silent, and I don't mind admitting that I'm afraid. I keep expecting someone to jump out of the shadows and catch me breaking the rules.

But no one does.

Daniel is in the art room, looking at one of the painting books, when I walk in. Even though he's expecting me, he jumps.

"I am not going to slide down the math hallway,"

I say. "And I really don't think Gerald would do well out in the wild."

He doesn't respond. Instead he blushes as he holds out a small, silver-wrapped box.

"I've given up on the list—for now," he says. "But I didn't want you to open this in front of anyone else, in case you hate it."

The last thing I expected was a present. It's not my birthday, and even if it were, I wouldn't expect Daniel to get me anything. My fingers shake a little as I open it.

Inside the box is a necklace with a little silver snowflake charm, which sparkles like glitter. Holy moly!

"Thank you," I whisper. "It's perfect."

Daniel beams.

Then he takes hold of my hand and walks me back to the gym. I don't object.

41

FORTUNES

Now it's Monday, and the necklace still hangs around my neck. Sasha has dance rehearsals all week, so I'm walking to Head Start alone. It's a warm May day, and I'm looking up — taking in the new green leaves, the cloudless sky — when something catches my eye. It's an airplane, a paper airplane, jutting out from a shrub. I gently pull it out and notice that this one's been folded from a report card. No doubt it's one of Reggie's planes and someone must want better grades.

In the same way that I used to look for pennies, I'm now looking for planes, and I find them.

An airplane in the gutter is folded from a letter. One next to a trash can is folded from a restaurant place mat. It's as if I'm on a treasure hunt and I can't stop looking! Wedged up against a building is yet another tiny plane, which has been folded from a dollar bill. For a moment, I'm tempted to take this plane, but I don't. I don't want to stop the wish from coming true.

All these wishes cast upon the wind.

They remind me of my deepest, most precious wish. *Maybe I should ask Reggie to help me fold a plane from a Carter application.* But I no sooner think of the possibility than I decide against it.

Here's why: wishing for one thing will wipe out lots of other possibilities. For example, if two months ago I had wished that Sasha and I would be best friends always, I never would have become friends with Daniel, and she never would have befriended Keisha. If I had wished to be patrol leader, I might never have worked so hard to reinstate the Eastland traditions. If I had wished that Gage and I got an apartment, I might be sitting home alone at nights while he went on dates with Chloe and worrying what would happen if he was late or if I locked myself out. And I would definitely be holding Gage back from having his own life, and myself from getting to be a kid. So I'm done wishing for something specific.

Instead, I'll wait to see what happens next.

42

PAGES

Everyone said that we would get our letters from Carter on Saturday. Mademoiselle Barbary said so, Marianna said so, Janna said so. So imagine my surprise when I get home on Friday and there is the letter on the counter.

Even though I can tell that Janna wants me to open it right away, I don't. It's an important moment, and whether I'm accepted or not, Gage should be here with me, too.

I call Gage, and he promises to hurry over right after work. In the meantime, Daniel calls to say he's been accepted.

"I didn't even know you applied!" I say.

"Yeah, I know," he says. "I wasn't going to, but something changed my mind."

Before I can ask him if it was *something* or *some-one* who changed his mind, he tells me that Keisha posted her acceptance online. I haven't heard from Sasha, and it's making me nervous.

When Gage finally arrives, I am practically jumping out of my skin. I open the letter and read:

Dear Ms. Hazard,

It is with great pleasure that we offer you a place at Carter Middle School for the next three years. . . .

Janna cries. I do, too.

I got into Carter. Despite the dip in my grades and the detention on my record. Despite telling the application people about my and Gage's time being homeless. Despite not wishing for it on Reggie's plane. Despite it all—or maybe, really, because of it all—I've been accepted.

. . .

We have a delicious dinner that Janna cooked, knowing that we'd either be celebrating or in need of consoling, and then Gage says that he has a present for me.

"How come?" I ask, realizing that it's the second present I've been given lately for no reason at all.

"I thought congratulations might be in order." He hands me a wrapped cardboard box, which is so light it feels almost empty. I break the curly ribbon, tear open the paper, and open the box.

Inside is a lone L.L. Bean catalog. I start to frown, wondering why he's giving me a new catalog for my Paper Things when I've told him that I no longer play with them. But then I realize that this isn't a new catalog. It's one I've seen before—almost four years ago.

I open the cover and flip through the pages slowly, my hands shaking. And there he is: Miles, running through the sprinkler! I keep flipping. And there's Natalie in her yellow dress, holding her toad! Untouched!

I lunge at Gage and give him the biggest hug ever.

"I couldn't stand it that those girls destroyed your Paper Things," he says. "I wish I could replace all of them, but I figured these two were the most important ones."

"I can't believe you found the same catalog!" Janna says.

"It wasn't easy," says Gage. "But I found a woman through craigslist who had boxes and boxes of catalogs in her garage. You would have been in heaven!" Gage tells me, smiling. "She was going to recycle them, but she never did. If you're interested, I bet she'd be willing to give you more."

I think about his offer, but like wishing on Carter, rebuilding my Paper Things collection just doesn't feel right. That folder represents a me that no longer exists. I'm not embarrassed of her, but at the same time, I no longer want to be her. I've moved on.

Still, I tuck this catalog away, grateful to have Miles and Natalie safe together.

Later that night, after Gage has left to go out on a date with Chloe, Janna gives me the scrapbook she's been making in my honor.

"You're old enough to choose what to include," she says.

And immediately, I think of the objects that I'll paste inside: Natalie and Miles; a penny or two; my ode to seat cushions; a pipe cleaner left over from Crazy Hat Day; and the script from my Louisa May Alcott presentation.

And my Carter acceptance letter, of course.

DIPLOMAS

Having a last name that's neither at the beginning nor the end of the alphabet is cool. At school, whenever we do things in alphabetical order, enough kids go before me that I can prepare, but I don't have to wait my turn forever. So when my name is called at graduation, I am ready:

"Arianna Jane Hazard, daughter of Nicholas and Georgia Hazard and Janna Delaney; sister of Gage Hazard."

Turns out that I had to fill out a form that told the announcer at graduation what to say. I chose to list all of these names. I see Gage grinning when they read his name, and I know he's pleased that I put him on the list. I walk to the podium, accept my certificate that says I have successfully completed six years of schooling at Eastland Elementary School, and turn to have my picture taken—by the school photographer and by Janna. I now have another photo to put in my scrapbook.

Once the ceremony is over, Janna elbows her way up to Mr. Chandler, I think to give him a piece of her mind for how he treated me during the traditions campaign. But Mr. Chandler breaks into a grin when he sees her, and I overhear him congratulating her on my acceptance to Carter Middle School. "You must be so proud of Arianna!" he says. "We certainly are!"

Janna looks completely flabbergasted, like the wind's been knocked out of her sails. But soon she's grinning, too, and laughing. I turn away, blushing in embarrassment. But it's a good kind of embarrassment—the best kind.

I worry that Sasha has overheard this conversation, but she's left my side and is talking with Linnie's family. Sasha was wait-listed, which seems so unfair. I told her that I really hoped she would get into Carter and that maybe she should ask Reggie for a plane.

"Actually, I'm not that bummed," Sasha insisted. "I know my mom really wanted me to go to Carter—and I wanted to be with you and Keisha—but I think I can be one of the stars at Wilson."

"Sasha, you're already a star," I told her.

I'm standing in the hall outside the auditorium with Gage and Chloe when Daniel grabs my hand. "Come with me," he says.

I let myself be tugged away.

"What is it?"

"You've got a promise to keep," he says.

"What promise?"

It isn't until we get to the gym doors that I understand. "Now?" I say. "In our caps and gowns?" But I'm laughing, because it's even better in our caps and gowns.

He pulls me inside.

The gym is dimly lit and every sound echoes.

I spot a big pile of blue mats tucked into a corner, but the bleachers have all been folded up against the walls.

"Looks like we have no way of getting up there," I say, surprised at how disappointed this makes me feel.

"Oh, no," Daniel says. "You're not getting out of it that easy!"

He leads me to one end of the folded bleachers and shows me how to climb them like a ladder. I place my hands where he placed his and pull myself up.

For some reason, the top of the bleachers feels higher with them folded than it does when they're open. I sit down carefully and scoot on my bottom until I'm at the edge, with my legs dangling above the mats.

Daniel, still standing, holds out his hand.

"I don't think I can do it," I say, feeling suddenly nervous.

"Of course you can. Think of everything you accomplished this year."

He's right. It's been one heck of a year—and if I survived all that, then I can definitely survive this.

I take a deep breath, reach up, and let him lift me to a standing position.

He looks at me.

I look at him.

"Ready?" he says.

"Ready," I say.

We hold hands and jump.

ACKNOWLEDGMENTS

I wish I were a cleverer author—one who could write an original and adroit acknowledgments page. But I know my limits; I know what I require. To achieve that end, I'd have to first ponder my thoughts aloud, no doubt boring the ears off my loving husband and grown kids, who are used to my random questions and muddled musings . . . but still.

I'd have to run the page past my dear friend and trusted reader Jane Kurtz. She'd praise the good bits, and gently point out all the dull, implausible, unearned parts. We'd have lively conversations about building the reader's appetite and the nature of voice. But one reader, no matter how skilled, is never enough.

So I'd likely turn to the participants in Pam Houston's summer workshop at Fine Arts Work Center in Provincetown, who'd generously share their first impressions and keep me from skimming over the hard emotions a writer must experience in order to tell an honest story. Pam would remind me to stay grounded in the physical, to record exactly what I see, to trust that the deeper meanings will emerge.

And I would just be getting started. None too soon, I'd turn to my insightful editor, Kaylan Adair, who would painstakingly tease from me all the underdeveloped ideas, vague scenes, and lost threads. She'd make brilliant suggestions—suggestions that come not only from her literary expertise, but her understanding of the human heart. She's extraordinary.

Enough already? Not likely! Kaylan would work with a team: editorial director Liz Bicknell, copyeditor Pamela Marshall, copy chief Hannah Mahoney, managing editor Katie Ring, designer Heather McGee, production controller Angie Dombroski, e-book editor Andrea Tompa, and in-house champion Susan Batcheller. Without their help I could not punctuate this sentence, let alone create art.

That's what I would do. I'd seek help from the very people who shaped *Paper Things*, who were incredibly generous with their time, their talent, and their support. Who were, in a word, amazing.

But never mind. I won't wish for cleverness. Instead I'm casting my own wishplane with the desire that all who participated in the making of this book know how very grateful I am.